CW00474197

A TANGLED WEB

A DCI PILGRIM THRILLER
BOOK 2

By
A L Fraine

Book List

www.alfraineauthor.co.uk/books

Acknowledgements

Thank you to my wife Louise for her tireless support and great suggestions, my kids for being amazing, and my family for believing in me.

Thank you to my amazing editor Hanna Elizabeth for her critical eye and suggestions, they're always on point.

Thank you to my fellow authors for their continued inspiration and help.

And finally, thank you to you, the readers, for reading my crazy stories.

You're all amazing.

Thank you.

Table of Contents

1

"I gave you everything! Anything you ever needed. And this is how you repay me? This is how you treat me, you bitch!"

Curled up on the bed, her arms wrapped around her legs and her back pressed against the wall, Olivia cowered. Her eyes were wet from the tears that ran freely as she hid her face. Her cheek stung, her side hurt, and she just desperately didn't want to get hit anymore.

"Look at me," he raged above her, but she daren't, she couldn't, and squeezed her eyes shut, hoping it would end. "God damn it, look at me Olivia, or I'll smack you so hard..."

Terrified, she raised her head and peeked above her arms at the young man standing before her.

Jacob locked eyes with her.

"You've brought this on yourself. You know that, right? This is your fault. You've treated me like shit, so this is what you deserve."

Unable to bring herself to speak, she merely nodded. She didn't really agree with him, of course, but she'd say anything to get him to stop hitting her.

"How dare you do that, Olivia! How dare you humiliate me! I don't ask much. Just a bit of loyalty in return for

5

everything that I do for you! I give you money and a home. All the clothes you could want, and all I ask is that you show me some GODDAMN RESPECT!" he raged, eyes bulging.

Raising his arm again, he tensed, about to strike her. Olivia stiffened, waiting for it as she buried her head.

"Fuck!"

The hit didn't come. She looked up. Lowering his arm, he breathed hard, staring at her. "You and Lily, you're not going out again, got it?"

She nodded quickly.

He grunted in frustration and turned away from her. "Stupid fucking..." he muttered, cursing under his breath as he stalked out of the room, slamming the door behind him, only it didn't shut, and sprang back, coming to rest half-open.

She listened to him go, walking off along the hall and then down the stairs, leaving her in relative silence. The house wasn't that quiet, though. Music played downstairs somewhere, and she could hear voices too.

But she didn't pay them any attention.

Hiding her face, Olivia felt the tension fall away from her body as the adrenaline faded from her bloodstream. Fresh tears fell, and she sobbed into her sleeves, letting the emotion of the moment drain away.

What had her life become? How had she ended up in this godawful mess? She hated it and wanted out. This was the final straw, and she knew she'd be better off anywhere else but here, even at her stupid-ass parents' house.

Literally, anything was better than this.

As she sobbed, her despair turned to anger, and she punched her mattress in pure frustration. She had to do something. She couldn't stay here anymore. There seemed to be no more good times to have here.

Sometimes she wondered how things had got this bad, but the truth was that it *had* been good, once. It *had* been fun and rebellious. She'd felt like a grown-up, like an adult, and not like a child anymore. She always hated that her parents had treated her like a baby and never let her do anything.

But Jacob had been different. He'd never treated her like a kid, or even as a teenager. He'd talked to her like an adult, like a peer. She'd loved that. She'd loved the money too, and how he'd bought things for her, taken her out, and shown her what life could be like.

Over time, she'd left her life behind. Her parents, her friends, none of them understood her, none of them knew what was best for her. They didn't love her or care for her. They hated her.

Or, that's what Jacob had told her and convinced her of over months.

At the time, she hadn't realised.

7

But then came the drink, and the drugs, and the violence, until she'd ended up here, isolated, alone, shunned even by her own parents. No one could help her now, not even Lily, her only friend in this place.

But the other night, at the club, she'd seen a new life, a life outside of this horror show.

She needed to get out.

Tonight.

Now.

"Hey, are you okay?"

Olivia looked up through her lank blonde tresses at the girl who was creeping into her room. She nodded, and then changed her mind and shook her head. "No, not really."

Lily grimaced, before turning and closing the door behind her as quietly as she could, then crossing the room to sit on the bed beside her.

Olivia looked up at Lily and smiled, grateful that she would risk leaving her room. Lily was usually such a nervous girl, always careful never to put a foot out of line and doing as Jacob and Vassili asked. And yet, here she was, risking a beating by coming to check on her. There was a strength in Lily that she kept buried deep, and hardly ever showed. Olivia found this small act of rebellion inspiring. Smiling at her friend, she drew strength from her and sniffed her tears back.

"Thank you for coming to see me."

"I heard what he did. Ooh, that looks nasty," Lily replied, frowning at Olivia's face.

"I'll be okay," Olivia replied as her cheek twitched where it stung with pain.

"Are you sure? I might be able to get some plasters and antiseptic cream later."

"Thanks, but I'm okay."

"So, he found out then?"

"Looks that way," Olivia replied. "I don't know what he knows exactly, other than we went to that club."

"That'll be enough," Lily replied.

Olivia nodded, but suspected it was more. She remembered that night clearly and fondly, and she also remembered who she'd met. She was sure that was the issue. But how did he know?

How did he find out what she'd done and who she'd met?

She'd kept her phone hidden from him. Out of sight, out of mind and all that, so he couldn't take it. So how did he know?

Whatever, it didn't matter. She knew what she needed to do.

"I need to get out of here. I can't stay here anymore."

"But you can't. He'll kill you. You can't just leave."

"And I can't stay either. I can't do it anymore. You should come with me."

"No."

"You must. You can't stay here. I don't want you to go through what I have."

"You won't get out the house," Lily protested. "Look, don't make such a rash decision right now. Sleep on it. Things will look better in the morning. I'm sure he'll apologise."

"Apologise? And that's meant to make it all better, is it? After what he's done?"

"We did break his rules, and you were very friendly with that man."

"I did nothing wrong," Olivia protested.

"I don't think he sees it that way."

"I don't give a shit how he sees it, I'm not his property, despite what he thinks."

"What're you going to do?"

"Leave. I... I can't stay here. I need to get out. He'll kill me one of these days."

Lily nodded solemnly. "Where will you go?"

"Away from here." Olivia pressed her lips together and looked at the door, listening hard, but couldn't hear anything. She knew where she'd go, she had a plan... of sorts. "I need to get moving."

Taking a breath, she slipped off the bed and reached underneath it, running her fingers along the underside of her

10

mattress and the slats that held it up, until she found what she wanted.

Grabbing it, she pulled out the phone with its cracked screen. She checked its power and then slipped the device into her pocket. "I'm going to meet someone."

"Who?"

She sighed, unwilling to say until she was well away from here. "Come with me," Olivia hissed.

"I can't leave," Lily protested.

"You know what he'll do to you."

"He might not do anything."

"You know he will," Olivia insisted.

"You go… if you must. But I can't."

She nodded, reluctantly accepting Lily's choice. She'd never make it out if she had to drag Lily along too. "I'm sorry."

"It's okay," Lily insisted. "I understand. I'll be alright."

Releasing a held breath, Olivia shook her head. "You have to do what you think is right, I guess."

"And so do you. When will you go?"

A steely resolve settled over her as she considered her options, but there was only ever one choice. "Now. I'm not staying in this dump one more second."

"You think you can get out? You think he'll let you? There's nowhere for you to go, and you know he'll come for you."

"I'd like to see him stop me," she replied. The house wasn't really a fortress or a cell. They had certain freedoms. Instead, Jacob, Vassili, and the others relied on threats both physical and psychological to keep them in line.

"No, Olivia, wait until later, when it's quiet."

"No way. I'm not sitting here waiting for him to come back and... do whatever to me again. No way. I need to get out," Olivia replied, her heart thumping against her ribs like it was trying to escape.

This house rarely got truly quiet. Someone was always here, always up. And then there was the possibility of Jacob coming back. The thought of him returning and hurting her or wanting sex or something again, made her skin crawl.

A shiver ran up her spine as she made up her mind.

She had to make a run for it now. She'd go crazy if she stayed here another moment.

Pulling a bag out from under the bed, Olivia lifted it onto the mattress.

"You packed already?" Lily asked.

"I packed last night, but then I chickened out," Olivia admitted, feeling frustrated at her own weakness. "I should have gone, but... I couldn't."

12

Lily nodded, her eyes searching around the room as Olivia turned and checked her bag. Everything was there. It wasn't heavy. She'd made sure she'd be travelling light, just in case she needed to leg it.

"Maybe I can help," Lily said looking up at her, her eyes hopeful.

"Help? How?"

"I'll distract them."

"And how will you do that?"

"I'll think of something," Lily answered, her core of steel revealing itself again.

"If you think you can. Don't do anything silly, though."

"You mean like what you're doing?"

Olivia raised an eyebrow at her friend.

"Sorry," Lily replied and then got up. "Let me check the hall." She walked to the door, opened it, and peeked outside. "It's all clear."

Crossing the room, Olivia nodded as she slung the bag over her shoulder. "Okay, good. I'm ready."

Pausing, Lily looked her in the eye. "Be careful, okay? And text me once you're out and safe."

"I will, and thank you," she answered, hugging her friend. "I'll miss you."

"I'll miss you more."

"If I can come back and get you…"

"I'm okay. Don't worry about me," Lily replied, wiping the tears from her eyes. "Now shut it, you'll just make me cry."

Olivia smiled warmly, her heart aching now that the moment had come.

"Let me go first," Lily said and stepped out onto the landing. Olivia reached the door and looked out as Lily started down the stairs. The music that echoed up from downstairs was noticeably louder, thumping through the house. The neighbours had learnt long ago not to complain.

Stepping out of her room, Olivia looked up the hallway, and then back into her room. She felt bad for leaving, but she couldn't stay.

Maybe once she was out of here, she could call someone, try to change things, and help her friend. Letting out a long breath, she moved to the stairwell and looked down.

Below, Lily glanced up and nodded before walking into the front room.

"Evening, guys," she heard Lily say. "What's up?"

Taking that as her cue, Olivia crept down the stairs, keeping her feet towards the sides of the steps where they didn't creak so much. Moving slowly and treading carefully, she winced each time she shifted her weight onto the next step, hoping it wouldn't alert anyone.

Halfway down, a step creaked.

She froze, hoping no one had heard her, but the music was loud, and after a few seconds, she felt sure no one suspected anything. No one should really, anyway.

Focusing on the hallway at the bottom of the steps, she pressed on, moving swiftly, until she finally stepped onto solid ground.

Taking a breath, she crept up the corridor, her eyes flicking between the entrance hall up ahead, and the door to her left.

Glancing back, she looked towards the kitchen at the back of the house. To her relief, no one was back there watching, so she pressed on.

As she passed the open door on her left, which Lily had pushed half-closed to try and conceal her escape, she caught a glimpse of Lily standing before the fireplace, apparently lost in the music and dancing slowly, sashaying her hips left and right.

Clever girl, Olivia thought and left her to it.

Reaching the deserted entrance hall, she approached the front door and found it left ajar. Olivia frowned. This wasn't right.

Gently, she pulled on the door, widening the gap, and looked through.

She stiffened as she spotted Jacob outside, puffing on a cigarette in the dull morning air.

Shit.

Frozen to the spot, she wasn't sure what to do and bit her lip as she considered her options. Backing away, she glanced back the way she'd come and could hear voices. No, she couldn't go back now. She had to get out of here. She had to just run for it. This was her chance, and she wasn't going to just turn around and slink back into her hellhole of a room.

Steeling herself, she grabbed the door handle and pulled it wide to find Jacob standing, facing into the house as he crushed his cigarette underfoot.

Surprised, Jacob locked eyes with her. "Wha...?"

Olivia returned his gaze and then charged at him, raising her hands and shoving him away with a grunt. "Ugh."

"What do you think you're..." Jacob exclaimed, and reached for her, grabbing her arm as she tried to push past.

"Aaagh, get off," she hissed.

"Where do you think you're going?"

"Away from you," she replied and stamped on his foot as hard as she could. He winced and grunted, but held on.

"Ugh, you'll pay for that." He tried to grab her with his other hand. Olivia fended him off, twisting and pulling herself around and away from him.

"Get off me."

"Come here, you..."

Rage built up inside her. She would never go back in that house, ever, not while there was still breath in her body. Almost entirely on instinct, Olivia balled her fist and lashed out, swinging at his face.

Jacob yelped in pain and let go of her, staggering back. Olivia fell and landed on her rear as Jacob held his face and dropped to the ground.

"Aaah, my eye. What did you do? What did you do?"

"What?" she gasped.

"My eye, you've blinded me you crazy bitch."

"But, I…" She looked down at her fist and saw blood on the ring she wore. For a second, a pang of regret flared in her mind. She didn't mean to really hurt him.

For a moment, she nearly went to him to check on the wound, and then reality slammed back into place, and she mentally scolded herself for still caring.

This was her chance. She could leave, and frankly, screw him.

"No less than you deserve," she said.

Jumping up, Olivia backed out over the front garden, up the drive, watching Jacob at the front of the house.

"Come here. Come back. Don't you dare leave! I'll kill you! Do you hear me? I'll find you, and I'll kill you!"

Turning, Olivia ran taking a left out of the driveway and sprinting up the street.

The day seemed to crawl by, as she counted the minutes and hours while waiting. Olivia had spent the day riding buses from Redhill to Epsom and then hiding in cafés and supermarkets, jumping at shadows as she prayed Jacob wouldn't find her.

Because she knew he'd be out there, somewhere, hunting for her. There was no way he'd let her just walk out like that. He'd warned her several times about leaving, and what he'd do to her if she tried.

She just hoped Lily would be okay.

But it wasn't just Jacob she had to worry about. Vassili and his bitch of a girlfriend, Yana, wouldn't be happy either, and in some ways, they were more dangerous than Jacob. But he knew her better, and might somehow guess where she'd gone. So it paid to be careful.

As night drew in, she'd finally set off through town, making for the large car park on the east side, behind the cinema. She'd agreed to meet there, and hoped she wasn't being led on.

She kept her head down and her hood up as she went, her eyes scanning the faces around her in case she saw Jacob, hunting for her.

It would be the height of irony to get this close to her meeting, this close to what she hoped was her salvation, and have it snatched away. But she couldn't think like that. She had to press on. She had to hope that this would work out.

Walking into the car park, she moved to the back, furthest away from the street, and looked around. No one seemed to be there, though, and she found herself alone amidst a scattered collection of cars in the darkness.

Finding a spot to stand and wait, not too close to any particular car, but away from the roads between the parking spaces, she pulled out her phone and checked her messages.

She was in the right spot and sighed. Maybe she was being stood up?

Tapping on her phone again, she brought up her messages and stared at the last conversation she'd had with Lily a couple of days ago before she'd left the house. She'd resisted messaging Lily all day, feeling somehow sure that Jacob would find out.

She wasn't supposed to have a phone. Jacob had taken them away a while ago. That hadn't stopped her and Lily from getting another one each, though, without Jacob and the others knowing.

She started pacing up and down, staring at her phone and pointedly ignoring the world around her. She didn't want to see anyone and didn't want anyone questioning her.

Keeping to herself and hiding her face had seemed like a good idea, but as it turned out, maybe not. She didn't see the figure approach and get close. She only became aware of them when they spoke. But by then, it was too late.

"Miss Olivia Cook?" a voice asked.

She looked up, just as something struck her across the head, and the world around her turned black.

2

Jon leant back in the passenger seat of the police pool car as they sped along roads, the siren wailing across the Surrey countryside as Nathan expertly navigated the roads.

"Have you heard about that conspiracy theory that the heads of government are reptilian aliens wearing skin masks?"

"I have," Nathan replied, guardedly.

"Do you believe in that one?"

Nathan smirked. "No, I don't think so, I'm not crazy."

"But, you think there are some secretive cabals influencing governments around the world, right?" Jon had heard the rumours about what Nathan believed.

"It's a thing," Nathan replied with a shrug. "There's that Skull and Bones group over in the States, right? You've heard of them?"

"Aye, I think so. Rich pricks with delusions of grandeur, right?"

"I suppose so. Then there's the Freemasons and others too. I don't know how much sway they have over government policy, but these kinds of clubs have been around for years. But, as for lizards in human skins? I don't think so."

"It all just sounds bat-shit crazy to me," Jon replied and could see why he'd picked up the nickname Fox from some of his former colleagues.

"Although," Nathan continued, "have you met Assistant Chief Constable Ward yet? Now, if ever there was an alien posing as a human, he'd be it."

Jon smirked. "I've not had the pleasure of meeting this wonderful sounding human being."

"Well, when you do, you might revisit your idea of what's human and what's not."

"You're not a fan, I take it?"

"He's just a bloody stick in the mud. One of those who didn't put in the time in the trenches. He came straight into the police as a superintendent."

"Direct Entry," Jon muttered, aware of the program.

"Yep. He's one of them."

"Okay. Well, I'm sure he's not that bad," Jon replied, feeling like he should defend his superior, even though he'd never met the man. He'd run across several officers that had walked into positions of power. While they did bring some valuable experience from outside into the service, they also hadn't spent time in the trenches, which sometimes led to issues, not least of which were conflicts of interest.

"Hmm. So, are you ready for tomorrow then, Loxley?" Nathan asked.

With a raised eyebrow at the nickname Nathan had given him, he looked over. Jon shrugged, doing his best to seem unconcerned that it had been over two weeks since he'd last seen Kate. "Aye. It'll be good to have her back."

"It will. I wonder how her finger's holding up?"

"The doctors seemed to think she'd make a full recovery when I last spoke to them. Still, I'll be sure to take the piss whenever the opportunity arises."

"I'm sure you will," Nathan replied with a smile. "That's good, though. We can't have an officer with a gammy pinky."

"I'm sure Barry the Finger will be fine. She's been signed off as fit for duty."

"You'll never be in her good books calling her that."

"She knows it's a sign of affection."

"Is that right? You're looking forward to seeing her again then?"

He was. After everything they'd been through with the Abban case, and the ordeal she'd suffered, it felt like he had a kind of connection with her.

Then there was the night they'd spent together, and her subsequent request to slow things down. He wondered what that meant for him?

For them?

They'd barely spoken for the last few weeks. She'd been staying with her parents while she recovered, and he'd respected her boundaries. They'd spoken briefly on the phone, swapped some messages, but he'd made a point of not talking about what had happened between them. She needed time and space, and he made sure she had it.

He didn't blame Kate for that, not after what had happened. She needed to get away, and she needed familiarity. She needed her family.

He and the rest of the team would only serve as reminders about that last case, something she didn't need while she recovered.

But she was coming back tomorrow, and he couldn't deny that he was looking forward to seeing her again. It felt like it had been an age since he'd visited her in the hospital.

"Aye, of course," he replied. The team didn't feel complete without her.

"She's a good detective," Nathan agreed, and then leant in closer to him. "But don't tell her I said that."

"I wouldn't dream of it. She'd only get a big head. So, what do you think we'll find when we get there?"

"It's a kidnapping, right?"

"Hostage situation," Jon clarified. "Some guy thinks his wife's been cheating on him and has them at gunpoint."

"Gunpoint? Christ, this isn't America."

"And yet, some days, it feels more and more like it."

"I can do without that. So, who's going to be on-site?" Nathan asked.

"There's already a team there, including some armed officers. We're there to mop up afterwards. I doubt this will take much investigation, though."

"Probably not. I'd like to say we'll find the situation resolved and the hostages alive, but I don't feel optimistic."

"That's the problem with you soft southern pansies, you need to lighten up and be a bit more positive."

"Piss off," Nathan protested with a smile. "I'm a positive person, despite what this job does to you, you northern gorilla."

"And yet, whenever I walk down the street and say hi to people I pass, you know, like a normal, friendly human being, I get dirty looks half the time."

"They're probably surprised to see the local zoo is holding open days and letting the animals out to wander the streets."

"I'm a gentle pussy cat," Jon protested, with a slight grin at his retort.

"You got it half right," Nathan quipped as they rounded the corner into the council estate, and saw the collection of police vehicles that had gathered in the street.

A wide cordon had been set up with the locals kept well away. A couple of the officers on duty let their car through the white and blue tape, and Nathan pulled up a short distance beyond it. Jon climbed out in time to see a team of armed officers run for the house up ahead.

"Looks like they're headed inside," Nathan stated.

"Nothing gets past you, does it, Fox?"

"Eyes like a hawk," Nathan agreed.

"Oh well, looks like we'll miss the fun," Jon stated as he approached the scene. As they walked, a uniformed officer turned to one of the others.

"The dicks are here," Jon heard him say.

The other officer, an inspector by the rank on his uniform, turned and then approached.

"Detectives?"

"Aye, we're the dicks," Jon replied, deadpan. "DCI Pilgrim and DI Halliwell."

"Good to have you," the Inspector replied, ignoring his quip. "We've just heard gunshots, so we're moving in. We'll get you in once it's all secure."

Jon nodded and stood back, letting the team finish their operation. Taking over now would only confuse matters at a sensitive moment.

But it wasn't long before the hostage-taker was subdued. Not long after, the all-clear was called, allowing them to move into the house and look over the scene.

Jon stood in the doorway to the back bedroom and surveyed the bloodbath that it contained. Two bodies lay sprawled on the floor, their blood soaked into the carpet and splattered up the wall. He felt intensely sorry for the ordeal they'd been put through, especially the child. That was no way to go, especially not at the hands of their father.

Turning away, he walked into the front bedroom where several armed officers stood guard over the man who'd caused all this death and destruction. He wore only trousers and lay on his front on the floor, his hands cuffed behind his back. The man glanced up at Jon, his blood-covered face scowling.

"Killed his wife and kid," Jon said to Nathan, standing nearby.

"Yep," Nathan replied. "Makes me sick. Sometimes I think I don't understand this world anymore."

"I've not understood it for a long time," Jon replied, thinking of his murdered girlfriend, Charlotte. "At least this should be a fairly open and shut case, and we can move onto something else. We know who did it, after all."

"She deserved it," the man on the floor spat.

"Oi, shut it, you," one of the armed officers said, and gave the man a nudge with his boot.

"No, you shut up," the killer replied. "I loved her, but she shouldn't have treated me like shit."

"Yeah, look at all that love splattered around that bedroom," Jon replied.

The killer grunted and looked away. "She deserved it."

"I doubt that, very much," Jon answered, done with him. He turned to the nearby officers. "Get him out of here."

"One of the men nodded and set his men on picking the guy up, when Jon noticed movement at the door. He looked up to see a figure step into view. She wore a fitted suit and had her auburn hair tied back in a ponytail.

"Kate?" Jon exclaimed, shocked. "Aye up, lass, what you doing back here?"

"Hey," she replied brightly. "I leave you guys alone for a few weeks, and you're already out here playing with guns?"

Jon smiled at her comment, only for a scuffle to occur to his right. He turned in time to be shoulder-barged by the killer who'd taken advantage of the distraction Kate had caused and slipped out of the grip of the two officers handling him.

He ran for the door.

"Hey," Kate shouted, launching herself at him.

She tackled him around the waist and knocked him flat on the floor, by which time Jon was back on him, restraining him with some of the other officers.

"No you don't, sunshine," Jon said as he helped hold the man down while they called for some extra hands.

He looked back up at Kate. "I bet you missed this, didn't you?"

"Oh yes, nothing starts the day off better than a coffee and a quick rugby tackle."

"With moves like that, you should join a women's team."

"Women's?" Nathan said from the other side of the killer, holding the man's leg down. "She'd flatten half the men's side with that tackle."

"I suppose it would mean I get my hands on some sportsmen," she replied, pulling a quizzical, but approving face.

"I knew you'd find the positives in it," Jon answered.

"Oh, you know me, I'm a glass-half-full kind of girl."

"That'd be a wine glass, right?"

She smirked and nodded as a few more officers walked into the room and took the killer away. Nathan followed them out, leaving Jon alone with Kate in the front bedroom. He watched Nathan go and then turned to her.

"So, how are you?"

"I'm okay," she replied with a smile, her dusky eyes twinkling. "Much better now, thank you."

"And the finger?"

Holding it up, Jon noted she wore a protective cover that wrapped around her wrist and came up over her little finger, which she curled and straightened for him, demonstrating her range of movement. "It's basically fine and healing well. The doctors are pleased with my progress."

"I doubt they'd be happy with you single-handedly tackling suspects, though."

"That's cute of you, Jon, but I'm fine."

"Good. I've er... I've missed having you around."

She nodded. "I've missed being here. So, um, how about we get something to eat later?"

He couldn't help the smile that spread over his face at her suggestion. "That sounds great."

"Jon," Nathan called back up the stairs. "The press is here, they want a statement."

"Arse."

3

"I'm sorry to say that the situation here today resulted in the deaths of both hostages at the hands of the man responsible. We won't be releasing their names at this time to give their families some privacy, but please rest assured that the man responsible is now in custody. I won't be taking any questions at this time, but further details will be released in due course. Thank you."

Sydney shifted her position in the chair, crossing her legs as she watched the news on the large TV, and the rather yummy police detective who was giving the press conference.

She smiled as she watched the rest of the news report with the anchor talking about the hostage situation that had played out this afternoon. It was nice to have a little bit of drama on an otherwise slow day.

As she sat pondering the future, Blake strode into the room, his eyes shooting daggers at her as he passed. He walked up to the TV and turned it off with a violent jab of his finger, before he stood up straight, and looked back at her.

"Good morning, Blake. It's another beautiful day," she said.

"If you say so."

"I do. Don't you agree?"

"With you? Never. What are you doing today? Lounging around, making the place look untidy, as usual? Or will be you spending Russell's money, again?"

"What I do with my time, is none of your business, Blake," she replied, narrowing her eyes as she looked up at him. Blake was a mountain of a man, and quite intimidating to most people. But then, she wasn't most people.

He was probably used to people being wary of him and doing as he asked, but she wasn't about to give him that satisfaction. Instead, she enjoyed defying him and showing him just how unimpressed she was by him.

He'd never lay a finger on her of course, and if he did, he'd live to regret it. Besides, Russell would never stand for such behaviour.

He knew that and so did she, and it frustrated him endlessly.

"It's always my business, Sydney. Anything that affects Russell is my business, and that includes you."

"Have I done something wrong?"

"Not yet, but I'll be there when you do, you can count on that."

"Be sure to tell me when that moment arrives, I wouldn't want to miss it."

"Oh, you won't. You're just another harlot interested in one thing only. I know your kind."

"That's really not very nice, Blake. Russell and I are very much in love. Surely, as his personal bodyguard, you can see that."

"There's a difference between infatuation, and love, Sydney. You're just the flavour of the month, that's all. Don't get comfortable."

"A month? That's a little pessimistic of you."

Blake narrowed his eyes and looked like he was chewing on a brick for a moment when she heard movement behind her.

"Morning Blake. I hope you're being nice to Syd."

"Good morning Mr Hodges. Yes, we were just discussing the weather."

"Of course you were," Russell replied, clearly unconvinced as he walked around the sofa, coming into view. Russell was a slim, handsome man in his ten-thousand-pound tailored suit and short dark hair. He leant in and kissed her briefly, placing his hand on her knee as he did so, giving it a squeeze. "Good morning, babe."

She smiled back at him. "Hey yourself."

Straightening up, he smiled down at her. "I hope Blake isn't bugging you."

"Oh no, he's just a big soft pussy cat," she replied, turning her smile towards Blake. "Aren't you, Blake?"

He turned away from her and focused on Russell. "Everything is ready for your day, sir. The car is fuelled and waiting for you."

"Thank you, Blake. Whatever would I do without you?"

"I honestly do not know, sir," he replied.

"Well then, shall we go?" He reached a hand out to her, which she took, allowing him to pull her up from the sofa. Interlacing her fingers with his, she walked out with him, giving Blake a sideways look, which he returned with a scowl.

It was at moments like this that she remembered that old proverb, 'May you live in interesting times.' She felt it captured the moment, perfectly.

4

Jon stabbed the chip, making sure it was fully covered with gravy, and stuffed it in his mouth, savouring the mix of salty potato and meaty sauce.

Mana from heaven.

Kate made a heaving noise from beside him as they sat perched on the bonnet of his Vauxhall.

Jon glanced left.

"I don't know how you can eat that," she commented. "Gravy? On chips? Is that a northern thing?"

"It's a beautiful thing, Pinky," he replied as Kate placed a chip in her mouth, only for her to smirk and then start coughing. Jon reached over and gave her a couple of solid pats on her back. "You alright there love?"

She took a moment to get control of herself before looking up, wiping her mouth with the back of her hand. "Pinky?" she asked, incredulously.

Jon raised his hand and wiggled his little finger at her.

"Genius," she muttered, sounding mildly offended but amused, and skewered another chip.

"I know, right? I just keep coming up with them. I'm seriously on fire down here. I think there's something in the water."

"Gravy, perhaps?"

Jon chuckled. "Nice one, Barry. Seriously though, I think there *might* be something in the water. I've had a dicky tummy for a while now."

"That'll be the hard water," Kate replied, as she munched on some cod. "I think you have soft water up your way."

"It'll be the only thing that's hard down here," he replied.

"We're all soft southern Nancys, is that it?"

"I didn't say it."

She sniggered. "I guess not."

"So, what do you think?" Jon asked and nodded to the house. "You've not commented on it."

Kate turned her head and looked up at the three-story townhouse, with its dark bricks and the For Sale sign out front. "Do you *want* my opinion?"

"Of course. You know the area better than I do, for a start."

She nodded. "Yeah, I like it. Guildford is a nice place to live."

Nodding, Jon smiled. "Good. Yeah, I kind of like Guildford. It's not bad for a southern city. I mean, it's no Nottingham or Mansfield, but..."

"It would need a much higher crime rate to be like either of those," Kate mused.

"Fair point," Jon replied with a smile.

"You seem to have become a little more friendly with Nathan, while I was gone."

"I suppose," Jon replied, thinking back over the last few weeks, during which he'd worked fairly closely with him. "The boy's got skills. I mean, he's bat-shit crazy too, but it's a good kind of crazy."

"A useful kind of crazy, for a detective."

"Mmm," Jon replied as he took a bite out of the battered sausage.

"Nice length," Kate asked, eyeing his food with a cheeky glint in her eye.

"Aye, it's not bad," Jon replied, deciding not to go for the bait.

"Well, as long as you and Nathan didn't miss me too much."

Jon nodded. "We missed you," he replied in a more serious tone, being honest with her.

"We?"

Seeing what she was getting at, he steeled himself. Were they going to talk about this now?

"I missed you," he answered, staring at his gravy-soaked sausage and chips. After a moment, he looked up, meeting her gaze. "I missed you a lot. But I'm pleased you've come back, especially after everything you went through."

"I'm glad to be back," she replied. "I've just been dealing with a lot recently. I'm sorry I've been away, but I couldn't stay in my flat. I needed some space and normality."

"It's okay. I understand. I think I'd have needed some time to myself too, if that had happened to me. In fact, I did take some time after Charlotte..."

"You understand," she muttered, smiling to herself as she looked away.

"I do," he nodded. "And look, I know things were tough, and you weren't yourself the other week, so if you want to call it a day between us, that's fine too. Things are all messed up, so I get that your head might not have been in a good place when we..."

"No."

"Sorry?"

"No, I don't want to call it off between us. But I have to say, the way I acted, that's not typical for me. I'm not usually so forward."

"That's okay. I'm sorry if you think I took advantage."

"No, absolutely not. You didn't. What happened, happened, and that's fine. But I'd kind of like to start again."

"Sounds good," Jon replied, understanding where she was coming from a little more, and finding himself agreeing with her. "I think I'd like that too."

"That's settled then," she replied with a smile.

"So, do you want to go on a date sometime?" Jon asked. She might want to take it slower, but he saw no reason to draw it out too long. Besides, if they were going to be dating, they might as well go on some actual dates.

Otherwise, what was the point?

Kate smiled. "You don't hang around, do you?"

"I'll take it as slow as you like, but that does imply that we're actually starting something."

She nodded. "No, you're right, it does."

"And this doesn't count," he added, pointing his wooden fork at the chips and the car they were sitting on.

"I'm glad of that, at least, Oxo boy."

"So, you're saying that chips on the side of the road, sitting on a car, isn't a good first date?" He raised one questioning eyebrow.

"I've been on better, let's say that."

"Well, I've never been so insulted in all my life. Up north, this is the height of sophistication, I'll have you know."

"I think you might need to try a little harder, Pilgrim."

Jon frowned and nodded several times. "I'll need to get my thinking cap on then."

"No pressure."

"Oh, no. None at all."

"So, shall we say, the end of the week?" she suggested.

"Perfect," he replied, feeling a small thrill and flutter inside at the thought of it. He couldn't help but grin and wondered if he looked like the cat that got the cream.

He rewarded himself with a few more chips and another bite of the sausage, enjoying its meaty goodness.

"I'm going to have to induct you into some other types of food though."

"I eat well."

"How about a salad?"

"Nah, none of that fattening green shit, thanks. I'm not a rabbit."

"I can see that. It's the ears that give it away."

"Observant. You'll go far, Barry."

"I'll need to come up with a better nickname than Loxley though, I think."

"I like that one. Makes me sound like some heroic member of Robin Hood's Merry Men," he said with an approving look.

"You are not Robin of Loxley, Jon."

"I liked it."

"Why am I not surprised? Oh, yeah, because 'men'. That's why," Kate mused aloud to herself. "So that was Nathan's idea, was it, to call you that?"

"I suppose. He just said it one day."

She made an affirmative sound as she bit into another couple of chips. "So, no major cases while I was away then?"

"Nothing much, no. That hostage situation was the highlight really. But you were there for the end of that. Other than that, it was just a couple of minor crimes and tying up the loose ends of the Abban case."

Kate sighed. "Thanks for that," she replied.

"Anytime."

Moments later, a car pulled up, and a woman walked over. "Sorry, got caught up at the office," she said with a smile.

"That's okay. We've been enjoying our tea."

"Um…?"

"Dinner," Kate cut in. "We've been enjoying our dinner."

"Oh."

"Sorry, he's northern."

"Aaah, I see."

"I know, it explains a lot," Kate said, conspiratorially.

"Oi! I'm right here, you know."

"Careful, I think it understood us," Kate mock-whispered.

"I don't need to stand for this."

"Freeze, its vision is based on movement," Kate continued, standing stock still, her eyes tick-tocking side to side.

The estate agent smirked.

"I don't know what *you're* laughing at if you want a sale," Jon said.

"Sorry," the woman replied. "Shall we head inside?"

"Yes, let's," Jon agreed, and pointedly followed the woman up the path at the front of the house.

"We don't normally show people around houses this late in the day," the woman said. "But I understand your job makes it difficult?"

"Yeah, it takes up much of my time."

"What do you do?"

"We're detectives," Jon replied as she opened the door.

The woman paused and glanced back, before pressing on and continuing inside. "Oh, cool."

"Don't worry, we're not investigating you."

"Good to know."

"Unless... You've not killed anyone, have you?" Jon asked.

"I think I'd remember if I had."

"You'd think, wouldn't you...?" Jon replied, as he stepped into the front room and took in the space. The house had been stripped bare by whoever had lived in it previously, and it needed some work. There wasn't even carpet.

"It's a bit of a fixer-upper," Kate commented from the doorway.

"But it's got massive potential," the estate agent replied with a keen smile. "You could turn this into a perfect home for you both."

Jon raised an eyebrow at Kate and smiled. "She's casting aspersions."

"Eh, yeah, we're not… Well, we are, but, I'm not, you know… if you get my meaning," Kate stammered.

"Not really," the woman replied with a fixed, slightly mad looking grin on her face.

"I'm not sure the professors at Oxford would understand that, Barry. Have you been drinking…? Again?"

Kate raised a middle finger to him, and then pointedly turned around and moved deeper into the house. A moment later, he heard her call out.

"Oh, Jon. The kitchen is right up your street."

Jon raised an eyebrow at the estate agent, who just grinned wider. "Um, shall we head on through?"

"Why not? Let's not keep Barry waiting."

"Um," she replied, looking confused, before dismissing it, and leading him out the room. "The kitchen is this way."

Kitchen cupboards lined the room's walls, and the floor was in good nick, but there were no appliances of any kind. Kate stood beside a gap where he guessed the oven had once been.

"Look, a traditional space for a northern cooker, otherwise known as a campfire." Kate looked particularly pleased with that zinger.

"Ah, well," the agent said, sounding flustered, "there's plenty of space for your own appliances."

"You could get some rocks from the local wood," Kate continued. "Place them in a circle here, you'd feel right at home cooking some ferret over an open fire."

"Ferret?" Jon folded his arms and shook his head with a smile. "Are you having fun? You look like you're having fun. Maybe too much fun?"

"That's not possible."

"I think it might be."

"Shall we take a look at the other rooms?" the agent suggested nervously and made her way out.

"I think we're making her uncomfortable," Kate said, stepping up to him.

"If you can't handle the heat, get out of the kitchen."

She smiled. "I've missed you, Jon. I've missed this."

He nodded, enjoying her closeness. "Me too."

She smiled at him and then walked past. A brief sting flared on his right arse cheek, as Kate winked at him over her shoulder. "Come on then, Loxley, let's see what else this house has to offer."

5

Olivia rose from the depths of unconsciousness and delirium, slowly and surely. She was lying on something and was cold and sore. Her head pounded.

It was as if she'd been in a fight.

As she shifted position, an intense soreness in her arm made her hiss with pain. She tried to pull her arm in close, but it wouldn't come, and a sharp stinging in her wrist made her stop.

Forcing her eyes open, she did her best to take in the room around her. It was dark, with only a small window high up in the pitched eaves to let in some meagre illumination from a full moon, casting a square of light on the wooden floor.

It looked like some kind of attic room, and she found herself propped up on a bed. Her right wrist was cuffed to the metal frame, and the sheets were stained and dirty.

The inside of her arm was red with several fresh puncture wounds up near her inner elbow joint. She covered the raw wounds with her free hand, not daring to look at them.

Pulling one of the sheets close, she noted the unidentified stains and stiff parts of the fabric. Something had been spilt on it and left to dry. She wasn't sure she wanted to think about what that might be.

With a grunt, she pulled on the cuffs again, testing them, but there was no give there at all, and it only made her wrist hurt more. Searching the frame, she wondered if there might be a weak point or a gap, but it seemed she was out of luck.

Her stomach gurgled and cramped with hunger, making her feel weak and shaky.

She couldn't remember getting here, and from the moment she'd been bundled into the back of that van in Epsom, there'd been precious few moments of clarity.

She could remember images of the room and the bed, pain in her arm, and a figure, a dark shadowy figure.

She shivered, tears pricked at her eyes.

Oh God, how did she end up here? How did she find herself in this mess?

Footsteps approached the room, getting closer until she heard bolts slide and the door swung open. A man walked in wearing a mask over his nose and mouth, with only his eyes visible. He paused just inside the door. She could barely make him out in the darkness, he could be anyone. He looked her up and down, his eyes greedy and cruel.

She'd seen looks like that before, back in that house, with Jacob and his cronies.

Under his gaze, she felt weak and vulnerable. He took another step closer, and the terror took her completely. She screamed as loud as her lungs could manage.

The man stopped and watched as she shouted and screamed, calling for help at the top of her lungs. After a few moments, she noticed smile lines around his eyes. Was he enjoying this? Then she realised it was a smile of pity, and he shook his head.

"No one can hear you," he said before he lunged at her.

"No! Get away!" she shouted and kicked. She caught him a couple of times and made him grunt.

Could she fight him off? Could she turn the tables? She kicked again. He grunted and lashed out, walloping her in the face. Her head snapped back and smacked into the bed's frame. Pain flooded her senses, and the world swam around her. She could feel herself being pulled around, something scraping over her skin, followed by the coolness of the air against her legs.

He was stripping her.

6

Lily sat up in bed, her head still spinning.

For a while, she just sat there, waiting for the world to calm the hell down and stop moving by itself. It was dark outside, but she had no idea what time it was or even what day.

Several minutes passed as she just took in the room around her, which was frankly a mess. But then it always was. This was nothing new.

She could hear music playing somewhere downstairs, but the house was otherwise fairly quiet.

Feeling a little better, she reached down the side of the bed and pulled her phone out of its hiding place. She'd messaged Olivia yesterday, once she was away from the house, but there'd been nothing since, despite having tried to call and sending several messages.

She called again, hoping she'd pick up, but the call didn't even connect, instead, she heard the now-familiar automated voice telling her that this person wasn't available. She ended the call.

Frowning, she felt a deep dark pit of worry open up inside her stomach as she wondered why she'd not heard from her. That was unlike her.

Lily gasped as a thought occurred to her.

Maybe she's back.

Getting off the bed, she staggered, nearly falling to her knees before catching herself as her head swam. She took a moment to steady herself, holding onto the bed.

Looking down, she saw track marks on her arm and wondered what cocktail of drugs Vassili had given her this time, and what might have happened to her while she was under the influence. That unknown terrified her, made her feel sick to her stomach. Is that what Jacob had done to Olivia? Is that why she'd suddenly had enough?

Shaking her head, she banished those thoughts and made for the door with renewed vigour, and stepped into the hall.

Olivia's room was still there, and still empty. It was also trashed.

She wasn't here.

A deep-seated loneliness and vulnerability gripped her as she took in the room.

Someone had come in here and smashed some of Olivia's things, throwing them on the floor and stamping on them. It was most likely Jacob who'd done it in a fit of rage after she'd left.

He'd been furious with her when he came back into the house, stomping around, slamming doors, breaking things, before he and a few of the other guys left to find her.

That had been the last time she'd seen Jacob. Was he still out there, somewhere, looking for her? Or had he found her, and taken his anger out on her?

Maybe Olivia was right. Maybe it was time to get out. Now that her friend had gone, the reality of what was happening to them started to sink in. She had no one to comfort her anymore, no one to tell her everything would be okay.

But it wasn't okay. Nothing was okay, or alright, or normal. Everything was a mess, everything was, quite frankly, fucked.

What on earth were they doing here, living this life? Olivia had seen the reality of it before she had. She'd told her that Vassili and the others were using them. They'd groomed them, drawing them into their circle with money and praise, giving them so-called freedom and liberty. But in fact, it was nothing of the sort.

It was slavery of the worst kind, and they were trapped in it. Vassili, Jacob, and the others, they knew where her parents lived, they knew of her and Olivia's families. They'd cut them off from their friends and all their lifelines, leaving them bereft and alone, so they only had each other and their abusers.

And once they had nowhere else to go, that was when the nightmare started.

With Olivia gone, the truth of it was laid bare before her, and she knew she couldn't stay here any longer. She had to get out. She had to risk it all, and find help.

Fuck them, she thought, and stormed out of Olivia's room and back to hers.

Where could Olivia be? she wondered. What could have happened to her to make her not message back? But the answers to that were many and varied.

Jacob, or Vassili, or Yana could have found her and even now were holding her captive, torturing her maybe. Or perhaps she was at her parents, who'd confiscated her phone? Or with the police, perhaps?

Any of those were a possibility, and that wasn't even counting options like Olivia losing her phone, or her meeting someone Lily was unaware of. No, she needed to get out of here and find her friend, and she needed to do it now.

Shit, she wished she'd gone with Olivia yesterday, it would have been so much easier. But there was nothing for it, she had to do this on her own.

Lily stuffed some items in a bag. A few clothes and other bits, before finally giving up and taking a deep breath as she stared at the door to her room.

This was it. This was the moment.

Steeling her nerves, she strode out and made for the stairs. Heading down, she saw no one in the hallway ahead and pressed on. Her luck was holding. As she approached the entrance hall, she stopped and looked back at the top of a cabinet. Amongst the stubbed out cigarettes, dirty glasses, and other crap, she spotted a set of keys.

Car keys.

She recognised them, having seen them around the house and being used for one of the cars outside. She knew which one too. Moving back, she went to grab them.

Movement up the corridor caught her attention as she got her hand to the keys. Yana stepped out into the hallway from the kitchen. Lily froze as the woman gave her a curious look.

"Lily?" she said.

Shit. Grabbing the keys, Lily turned and ran. She dashed for the door, which was mercifully only on the bolt. Grabbing the knob to unlock it, Yana suddenly grabbed her from behind. Lily lashed out, her bag flying open and its contents spilling across the floor. Stumbling into the cabinet against the far wall, Yana fell away. Lily spotted her phone bounce on the floor, but there was no time to lose as Vassili's cruel bitch steadied herself.

Opening the door, Lily charged outside as Yana shouted for her from close behind.

"Lily, don't you... Jesus fucking Christ, who didn't lock the door again?"

Sprinting, Lily aimed for the car she knew the keys were for, clicking the unlock button as she went.

The car's side lights flashed as the locks slid into their housings. Slamming into the side of the car, she pulled the door open and jumped in. Shit, she was in the passenger seat. Lily reached for the lock button and pressed it. The car secured itself and not a moment too soon as Yana appeared at the window and started to yank on the door, screaming at her.

"Lily! Get out of this car right now! I mean it. Open the door."

Lily climbed over into the driver's seat and inserted the key.

"Don't you start that car," Yana shouted.

Lily ignored her and twisted the key. The engine roared into life.

"You bitch! You ungrateful cow. I'll find you. You can't hide anywhere. You hear me? We'll hunt you down, no matter where you go."

Lily dared not look at her. She didn't want to see that woman's face, contorted in rage, screaming at her. She only wanted freedom.

She slammed the car into reverse and backed out. Smashing the gates open she realised a little too late that she wasn't looking for oncoming traffic. Lucky, no one was close by and she bumped into the road without issue. Changing gears with a crunch, partly out of fear and partly out of unfamiliarity with driving, she looked up to see several men stepping out of the house, and Yana standing at the end of the driveway, still shouting.

With another attempt, she finally got the car into first and drove off. Heading into the warren of back streets, hoping she'd lose them, and keep her freedom.

7

Stood in the bathroom on the second floor at Horsley Station, Jon fixed his shirt in the mirror, wondering what would be best. Tie, or no tie?

He didn't really like them, most of the time. They got in the way and made for a convenient way for a criminal to grab him. But he also had standards to keep, and so relented, and put it on for now, keeping it loose. He hated the feeling of something tight around his neck.

Besides, this wasn't the only reason why he was fussing over his outfit today, if he were being honest with himself.

Looking around the house last night with Kate had been fun, and the property itself was exactly what he wanted. So this morning, he'd called up the estate agent and put an offer in for it.

Some of the rooms were in a better state than others, and it needed work generally, but the price was cheap, and it wasn't as if he was going to be spending much time there anyway. It was a place for him to sleep before he returned to the office, and that was about it, really. Besides, he liked the idea of a project. Something to keep his mind busy when he wasn't working.

There'd been a certain bittersweet feeling when he'd put the offer in, after leaving his old house in Nottingham behind. The house that he'd shared with Charlotte.

Now he was buying somewhere new, with the money they'd saved, and she couldn't be there. The thought made him sad, but he'd always known that he'd get a new home eventually. He couldn't spend the rest of his life renting that place.

The memories of Charlotte were just too strong there. He'd needed a break. He'd needed to get away from his old stomping ground and start afresh. It was a realisation that he'd only recently come to, after spending a few weeks down here, away from what he'd previously considered home.

He was now more confident than ever that this had been the right thing to do.

He'd needed this.

Satisfied with the tie, well, as much as he was ever going to be satisfied with it, he walked out and checked his watch. Their shift was about to start, and his team would be making their way into work.

He walked around to the break room and pulled a mug down from the cupboard as he set the kettle to boil. Reaching for the tea bags, he stopped and looked at the pack of loose leaf tea.

He felt like he almost wanted to hiss at the thing, like a Vampire at a cross. But with a force of will, be pulled the bag down and went through the motions of what he guessed was a more traditional method of tea making. It felt overly complicated and fussy to him, but he did it anyway, and before long, he had a pot of tea brewing away on the counter as he stared at the mug, holding the carton of milk in his hand.

This was all kinds of wrong.

Just the thought of putting the milk in first threatened to send him into a fit. That would make for a nice welcome back for her, wouldn't it? For Kate to find him lying on the floor, frothing at the mouth, babbling about the milk going in first.

Amused, he launched himself into the task at hand and poured some in.

Was it enough? Was this right for the amount of tea? It felt right, but he couldn't be sure. Maybe he could have timed himself pouring it out. How did she do this?

Suddenly hearing the first members of the team enter the room, Jon shrugged and poured in the tea. Within moments he knew he'd messed up. It was too strong. Not enough milk.

"See," he muttered to himself, in repressed frustration. "This is what happens when you try to be nice. How does she even do this? It's madness."

Jon went back and forth between pouring in a bit more milk, and then tea, and then milk.

By the time he'd finished, the mug was overflowing, but the colour was perfect.

"By heck, never again, Jon. Never again. Stick to what you know," he muttered to himself, before tipping some out into the sink and wiping the side of the mug.

"Having fun?" Nathan asked.

"Oh, oodles and oodles of it," Jon replied, turning to him. "I'm exhilarated. Can't you tell?"

"Oh, sure. I can see," Nathan replied sarcastically.

He sighed. "I don't think I'll ever know how she does this."

"It's magic, clearly. Still, that's a nice gesture, though."

"I know, right? I'm just trying to be nice."

"Did you have a look at that house then?" Nathan asked as he followed Jon over to Kate's desk.

"Yeah, I did. It was nice. The price makes my eyes water, and I think I might have a heart attack when the first mortgage payment comes in, but I'll have Valium on standby."

"What do houses go for up north? Tuppence and handshake?"

"Something like that. I've put an offer in though, so we'll see, I guess."

58

"The market moves pretty quick down here... Kind of like how you did with Kate."

"Takes two to tango, mate," he replied, placing the mug of tea on the coaster beside Kate's keyboard.

"I know. Still, you two got close pretty quickly."

"Not jealous, are you?"

Nathan laughed. "No, not at all. I'm not interested in her in that way. But I also don't want to see her get hurt."

"Neither do I," Jon replied, looking up at him. "And I think you should know that about me, by now."

"I do, I know."

"Good. So how's the hostage case coming along?"

"Just fine, the idiot hasn't got a leg to stand on, so all being well, he'll be going down for the murder of his wife and child. The media is already having a field day. You don't get away with killing kids."

"Good, he deserves everything he gets." Jon looked up to see Kate walking in, making for her desk.

"Good morning guys. How are my two favourite men?"

"Two, favourite?" Jon asked. "Now, come on, surely it's no contest?"

"I agree," Nathan replied. "I mean, I've known her longer, so clearly it's me."

"It's not the time, Fox, it's the mileage."

"Aww, who made me tea?" Kate asked.

Jon smiled. "I think that might edge it," he said, giving Nathan a smug look.

"Thank you," Kate replied, taking a sip. "Mmm, not bad."

Grabbing something from his desk, Nathan handed a packet to her. "Welcome back," he said. It was a pack of Fig Rolls.

"Oh, he's got a secret weapon," Kate said with a smile at Jon, before turning back to Nathan. "Thank you."

Nathan smiled over at him, and Jon looked from him to Kate's rapturous expression as she looked at the packet and then hugged it to her chest.

"You do realise," Jon said, looking up at Nathan, "this, of course, means war."

Nathan laughed.

"Now now, boys, no fighting over me."

"Morning," DS Rachel Arthur said in greeting as she wandered over. "Good to see you back, Kate. These two reprobates aren't bothering you, are they?"

"Nope. Good to see you too," she said, hugging Rachel and swapping some brief pleasantries.

Turning to Jon, Rachel said, "We've had a walk-in this morning, and I wondered if you wanted to take it?"

"What is it?"

"It's a girl claiming her friend's gone missing. Her name's Lily Austin."

"Sure, I'll take it," he said and took the file that Rachel handed him. Jon turned to Nathan. "You alright dealing with the hostage case?"

"Yeah, I'll be done with it before long."

"Great. Kate, are you feeling up to this?"

"Ready and raring to go."

Jon nodded, and led the way to the interview rooms downstairs. There they found the girl, Lily, sitting in the room with another woman, who they'd been informed was a social worker who was acting as the girl's responsible adult.

"Good morning," Jon greeted them.

"Hello, I'm Evie Gill," the social worker said with a smile, and offered her hand.

"DCI Jon Pilgrim and this is DS Kate O'Connell," he replied to the rotund woman, giving her hand a shake. Kate did the same.

"Nice to meet you," Evie replied.

"Lily, is it?" he asked, checking her name on the file.

She sniffed as she looked up through tear-filled eyes, and then looked over at Evie.

"It's okay, you can answer."

"Oh, um, yes," she said, looking back at John.

"That's good," he replied and explained what was about to happen. Once the formalities had been addressed, Jon let Kate take the lead, and got ready to take some notes.

The girl, who was apparently sixteen, looked quite upset. Aware of how intimidating it could be to have a man like him question her, he thought it best to hang back at first.

"So, Lily, why are you here today, what brought you to us?" Kate began.

"I just, I had nowhere else to go."

"Right, what do you mean?"

"It's my friend, Olivia. She's gone missing, and I can't seem to contact her."

"Alright, and when do you think she went missing?"

"The night before last," she replied.

"And how do you know this?" Kate pressed. "She might be home with her family."

Lily stifled a brief incredulous smirk and then briefly sobbed once. "We've been living together for months now, at... at a friend's house. She needed to get away, but she said she'd message, but didn't, and I can't seem to call her now either. The calls won't go through. That's not Olivia, she wouldn't do that."

"Wait, hold up," Jon said, leaning forward, unable to let that go. "You're sixteen, right?"

"That's right," she replied.

"And you don't live with your parents?"

"Um, no. I've not lived with them for a while now."

"Okay," Jon replied and flicked through the file. There wasn't much in here. Nothing about Lily or who she was. Just the report from the officers who'd brought her in early this morning, and what she'd said.

"I didn't get along with them, but I was friendly with Olivia who was friends with these guys who we ended up moving in with."

She said it like it was no big deal, which he supposed, it wasn't on the face of it. There was nothing against the law here, but something felt off. He had the distinct feeling that she was leaving out whole reams of information.

"These guys? Who are these guys?"

Shifting in her seat, Lily looked uncomfortable. "Just some friends of Olivia's. Jacob was her main friend. Her boyfriend I suppose. He invited us to live with them. It was great for a while, but Olivia has fallen out with him, and..." Lily leaned forward, and fought back the tears again.

"Just friends, were they?" Jon asked.

"Yeah."

"And this is Jacob's house you've been living in?"

"Erm, no. It's not *his* house, but he lives there, with Tyler and Zack and Yana, and..."

"Right," Jon replied, a note of incredulity in his voice. The more Lily spoke, the crazier it all sounded. What on earth was going on?

"Okay," Kate picked up the thread. "So you've lived with her for a while, and she's fallen out with her boyfriend. So, wouldn't she just go to her parents?"

"No," Lily replied. "She hates her parents."

"Is it not worth checking?"

"I did. That's what I've been doing all night. I went there to ask them for help, but they don't like me, so…" She shrugged.

"And Olivia wasn't there?"

"No, I'm sure of it."

"Right. Well, I don't think we've had a missing persons report filed in the last few days, but we can check that out." Kate looked at Jon as she spoke.

He nodded back to her and then addressed Lily. "So you have Olivia's number on your phone?"

"No. Well, um, yes, but I lost my phone. I dropped it."

"You dropped it? Where?"

"In the house."

"Oh, ok," Jon replied.

"So, is this Jacob worried about her too?" Kate asked.

"I don't know. He was angry with her. He… um. He hit her."

"He's attacked her?"

Lily nodded. "He hit me too."

"He's not such a great friend then, is he?" Jon remarked.

"I'm worried that he might have found her, and really hurt her."

"We understand," Kate replied, but Jon was perplexed. Surely she should have led with that bit of information? But so far getting anything out of her had been like getting blood out of a stone.

"That's why she wanted to run away," Lily continued. "It's why I left too. I couldn't stay there any longer, not without Olivia."

"So, why did he hit her? Did he say why he was angry?" Jon asked.

"I think it was because we went to a club the other night without them. We were all out together, but we got separated, so, Olivia wanted to have some fun and go to a club."

"And he didn't like that."

"No," she replied.

"He has no right to do that to you," Kate said.

"I know," Lily replied, sniffing back more tears.

"It's okay," Evie said. "You're doing well."

"So, where is this Jacob now?" Jon asked, feeling like he needed to have a word with the asshole.

"I don't know. I've not seen him since Olivia left the house. He must be out looking for her, or..."

"So, where's the house you lived at? Do you have an address? I'll need the full names of this Jacob and his friends too."

8

"So, what's your assessment?" Jon asked Evie in the quiet of the side-room.

"She's traumatised," Evie began, her eyes switching back and forth between him and Kate from across the table. "She's been through a horrific series of events, and it's going to take a long time to fully unpack. She's going to live with this for the rest of her life."

"Is it just violence?" Kate asked, "Or are we talking rape here as well?"

"I don't know. Right now, she's not telling me much, and she's focusing on her missing friend. I can't rule out violence, sexual violence, or drug abuse. My guess would be that it's a cocktail of all of those things, and she could also be blocking stuff out. I'll refer her to some specialists who will be able to work through this trauma with her, but don't expect to get all the answers you want in the timescale you need them. She might not remember some of it until years down the line, and if drugs were used, it might never come back. But what is clear is that she needs help and support."

"I understand," Jon replied. "I've worked a few cases like this before. Thank you, Evie, give her whatever she needs."

"I'd like to keep her here for a little longer today, she seems to feel safe here."

"That's fine. We'll probably have more questions for her anyway, provided that she's okay to answer them."

"She seems to want to help for now, so I'm sure that will be ok."

"Good. Her parents are in, I think, so I'll go and talk to them shortly, and when Lily feels up to it, I'm sure they'd like to see her."

"I'll talk to her," Evie replied, and left them to their work.

***

"Lily's run away from home a few times," Dion said, pointing out the reports in the file that Jon held as they walked through the station. "Seems like she was something of a rebel for a while. Olivia too. We have several reports of her running away, plus some petty crime too. The last report was just under a year ago. Lily's parents kept in touch, but Olivia's seemed to give up."

"Right, so Lily's been a bit of a handful for her parents, it seems."

"Looks that way. She doesn't have a record though, she's not been in any trouble with us."

"What about this Jacob Cole, and the others?"

"We're looking into them now, but a quick check confirmed a criminal record. Petty stuff mainly. I'll get the full report to you as soon as I can," Dion replied.

"Good work," Jon said. Dion nodded, and walked off, leaving him and Kate in the hallway.

"What do you think so far?"

"She's not telling us everything," Kate replied.

"That much is obvious."

"I don't like it. I want to know what she's hiding. And as for Olivia, I think we need a little more to go on."

"I agree. I'm not about to assign loads of resources to this yet. It's only been a day since her apparent disappearance, the latest of many, and we need to look into Olivia a little more first."

"I think you'll find another rebellious teenager," Kate replied.

"Oh, I know. But, aren't all teenagers like that? I remember hating some of the things my parents did back then. You must have rebelled at some point?"

"No. I was a good girl."

"I don't believe a word of it. I bet you were a right tearaway."

"Me? How very dare you. I was a model child."

"Ireland," Jon replied, referring to her teenage adventure when she tried to hunt down the killer of her aunt.

"Meh," Kate replied with a shrug.

"Thought so. We've all got skeletons in our closets, it's just that some are more horrifying than others. Right then, let's go say hi to her parents, they're downstairs."

Kate nodded and followed Jon down to the ground floor, and into a side room where two adults awaited. The woman, Lily's mother Jon guessed, was pacing back and forth in front of the man who was sitting on a sofa.

He stood when they entered, though.

"Is she okay? Is Lily here?" the woman asked, while the man stayed silent, waiting.

"Before I answer that, can I just confirm that you're Myles and Nina Austin?" Jon asked.

"Yes, of course," Nina replied and passed him some ID, which he checked and confirmed.

"Very good. Okay, I'm DCI Pilgrim and this is DS O'Connell, and yes, she is," Jon replied. "But, we just want to have a chat with you before we bring her down. Okay?"

"What has she done?" the man asked.

"Nothing," Kate replied. "She came to us for help. Her friend has gone missing."

"Oh?" he asked.

"Olivia?" the woman asked.

"That's the one," Kate confirmed.

"Lily came here this morning," Jon added, "because her friend, Olivia Cook, has gone missing from the house they were living in."

"Ugh," the man grunted. "Her again? She's nothing but trouble that one."

"Myles," Nina admonished him. "Let's not jump to any conclusions. So, what happened?"

"Well, firstly, are we right in thinking that Lily ran away from home about a year ago?"

Nina nodded. "She'd been going missing for several years before that though. She was always a handful. Olivia encouraged her I think too. She last went missing just after her sixteenth birthday. We filed a report with the police, but we just couldn't find her. We did get some messages from her though, saying she was okay and to stop looking for her."

"More like abusive texts," Myles added. "There was nothing friendly about them."

"Just stop it, Myles. If she came to the police, then clearly she needs help. I want to help her."

Myles sighed but said nothing.

"Well, she came to us today, because of Olivia. They've been living together, and Olivia recently went missing."

"Why?" Nina asked.

"Apparently, one of the young men she was living with hurt both of them, and Olivia seems to have had enough, so she left."

"Someone hit Lily?" Nina gasped.

"She's okay," Kate added. "But she will need your support. You have to understand, she's been through an intense, traumatic experience. Something that she may never fully recover from, and something that can, and likely will, flare up from time to time."

"You'll need to be there for her as she works through this. She's going to need professional help."

"My God, what happened to her?"

"We don't know the details," Jon replied. "She's not told us everything. She's focusing on her missing friend."

Myles rolled his eyes.

"What she doesn't need, are your opinions of Olivia," Jon said, looking at Lily's father. "They're not helpful. She needs your full support."

"Of course, anything," Nina replied. Myles nodded too, his bolshiness gone following Jon's words.

"I'm sorry. Yes, of course. I'll help her."

"Okay, that's good. We've got some investigating to do, so we're going to need you to stay here for a while. But we'll have some questions for you all before long."

"That's fine, thank you," Nina replied.

"We'll bring her and her social worker in," Jon said, and Kate went to get her. They walked in moments later. Lily looked cautious and shy, but her mother just hugged her and promised everything would be okay.

Satisfied that everything seemed to be going well, he left the room. He'd be back down later, but for now, the family just needed a little time.

"It's always nice to see family members being reunited," Kate commented as they made their way back upstairs.

"Aye. I just wish it happened a little more often," Jon replied. "We see far too much death and pain in this job."

"What do you think's happened to Olivia?"

"Hopefully nothing. I'm still hopeful that Lily is wrong and that she'll be hidden at her parents' house or somewhere."

"That would make for a nice change," Kate agreed.

"Which means this will likely turn into a multiple homicide case or something."

"Yeah, that would be just our luck," Kate replied as they returned to the SIU office.

"So, what have you got for us, Rachel?" Jon asked.

"Well, it turns out Olivia was a bit more of a tearaway than Lily was. She's got a small criminal record, mainly for theft and drugs offences, she's also been reported missing by her parents, Geoff and Sylvie Cook several times throughout the years."

"Just like Lily," Kate commented.

"In some cases, exactly like her. Some of them happened around the same time, as if they went missing together."

"Which they probably did," Jon muttered.

"Like Lily, the final report was from a year ago, but unlike Myles and Nina, Olivia's parents didn't follow up as much. It looks like they just gave up," Rachel said.

"They'd finally had enough?" Kate mused.

Rachel shrugged. "Other than that, I'm not sure there's much here, really. There's no new report on her going missing, so Olivia could be anywhere," Rachel said.

"There's an abuse case to be looked into," Kate suggested.

"True," Jon agreed. "But Olivia has a track record of going missing and then turning up later. Apart from the fact that Lily's not with her, this doesn't seem much different."

"She's got previous," Rachel agreed.

"I know, and yet, something's not right here," Kate answered.

"Got a feeling in your blood?" Rachel asked her.

"Something like that."

"Me too," Jon agreed. "I've definitely got a feeling."

"It's probably that gravy," Kate replied.

9

"So what else do you have for me?" Jon asked, sitting at the table in the office with Kate, Dion, Rachel, and Nathan.

"We've been looking into the house that Lily told us about," Nathan replied. "She was right, it's not owned by Jacob, but by a man called Vassili Syomin. He's a Russian National living in the UK. He's got dual passports and has been here a while racking up a nice little criminal record for himself over the years. He's mainly been trafficking drugs, and most of the offences we've charged him with are related to that. But I think there's more to him than just being a drug dealer."

"Oh?" Jon asked. "Been doing some digging, have you, Fox?"

"A little. He's managed to escape any serious jail time, mainly because of his lawyer, who's got some serious weight behind him."

"What kind of weight?"

"He's a Russian Mafia lawyer, and you don't hire a mob lawyer if you're not linked to them somehow."

"So, he's got links to the Bratva? Shit. What have we stumbled onto here?"

"I don't know. It might be that Olivia and Lily know nothing about all this, but then, maybe not," Nathan answered, with meaning filling his words.

"Crap, what if Olivia found out something she shouldn't have?" Kate mused.

"Then the Mob would not be happy," Jon replied, filling in the blanks.

"That's a leap," Nathan said. "It's far more likely that Lily and Olivia are just victims, and this is more of a lover's tiff between Olivia and Jacob."

"So, how does Jacob Cole fit in?" Rachel asked.

"Although, it does look like Jacob is working for Vassili, I think that's as close as he gets to the mobsters," Dion answered. "I think he's just a low-level cog in a much bigger machine."

Jon nodded and sat back in his chair. Memories of a case from a couple of years ago returned unbidden to the forefront of his mind, along with the fallout that resulted from it. It wasn't a case he liked to think about too much. But what he did remember, was the viciousness and cruelty of the Russian gangsters.

Mafia men were cold and cruel wherever they were from, of course, but this was one case he remembered more than some others, mainly because of the group's carefree attitude to human life.

Still, his previous experience with that criminal fraternity might be of use in this case.

"I've had some previous dealings with the Russians," Jon spoke up. "It was a money laundering and human trafficking case up in Nottingham, and they were a tricky group to deal with."

"Do you think they planned on trafficking Lily and Olivia?" Kate asked.

"I have no idea. Lily's not been very forthcoming, though, so maybe, but maybe not. This could just be a simple case of abuse," Jon replied.

Kate nodded.

"Okay, so this house where Lily was living with Olivia. It's owned by Vassili, and with his links, this could be a front for some of their activities," Jon suggested.

"I agree," Nathan replied. "There have been sporadic complaints from their neighbours, but they often withdraw them, which makes me think Vassili has been intimidating them into keeping their mouths shut."

"Okay, but all this is speculation for now. There could be nothing there, so I'm not about to go breaking down their door just yet. But I think it might be worth a quick house call to see what shakes loose. We need to focus on Olivia for now, though, so keep digging while Kate and I go and have a word with Vassili."

"Will do, Guv," Dion replied, and they all got up from the table, and went about their business, with Kate grabbing her jacket from the back of her chair as Jon made his way outside with Kate following on his heels.

"What are you thinking about?" Kate asked as they made their way outside, and into the waiting pool car.

"I'm thinking that my initial assessment, where I said I wasn't prepared to put resources into this, might have been premature," he answered, getting into the car and driving off with Kate in the passenger seat. "There's more to this than just a missing person case."

"Yeah, I have the same feeling."

"These mafia connections are worrying," Jon remarked after a while. "It could make things a lot more complicated."

"Organised crime has a way of doing that," Kate agreed. "But I'm not sure that Olivia and Lily were mixed up in that side of things."

"I hope not. Those guys are ruthless."

"You'll get no argument from me there. So, what do you hope to accomplish with this visit?"

"Honestly, I'm not sure, but I'm hoping we get to see Jacob. If we can find him, and ask him some questions... Who knows, maybe Olivia will be there too."

"I think that's a long shot."

"Yeah, probably."

"So, you had Russian Mobsters up north then?"

"Oh aye, we're all fancy up there, you know. We get all the best people coming to Nottingham."

"Sounds like it," Kate replied as they drove on through the Surrey countryside, heading east towards Redhill, and the house that the girls had been living in. "You know, I have a bad feeling about what these guys were doing with Lily and Olivia."

"Me too. It was nothing good, that's for damn sure."

"I think they groomed them and were using them, sexually."

"The thought had crossed my mind," Jon agreed. "I think these two girls only remained strong while both of them were there, but when Olivia left, Lily realised she couldn't stay. She realised the truth of the situation."

"That's nightmarish," Kate replied.

"I dread to think what they've been through," Jon said, as they drove into Redhill and made their way over to the estate. The house was located on a reasonably busy backstreet, a kind of rat run through this side of town where the locals cut through to shave seconds off their journey. The sizable house sported a wall, a hedgerow, and a set of dented gates to keep trespassers out.

It wasn't the biggest house he'd seen since coming down here, the Miller Gang's boss's house was much more impressive, but this was nice too. Or, had the potential to be, he thought as he walked up the driveway with Kate.

The garden was a mess. Amongst the uncut grass, there were piles of rubbish, some discarded wood, and other detritus piled up here and there. Vassili wasn't taking care of his property, it seemed.

"Hmm, not keen gardeners then," Jon commented.

"They probably have bigger concerns," Kate agreed as they approached the door.

"They need to get that grass cut," Jon remarked. "There could be a body in there, for all we know."

"It's grarss, not grass," Kate replied, drawing out the 'are' sound in her preferred pronunciation.

"I think you'll find there's only one R in grass, not two."

"I'll soon have you talking properly, you'll see," Kate replied.

"I do talk proper-like, love," Jon replied with a wry grin.

They used the doorbell, and before long heard the locks being undone before the door opened. The woman on the other side didn't pull it very wide though, only enough to show her face. She was probably in her late twenties, and there wasn't much that was remarkable about her, other than her cold blue eyes that flicked between Jon and Kate.

"Yes?"

"We're here to see Vassili," Jon began, noticing an accent.

The woman narrowed her eyes. "Who?"

"Vassili, the man who owns this house. Can you get him please?"

"There's no Vassili here," she answered in a now clearly Russian accent and moved to shut the door, only for Jon to put his foot in the way.

Pulling out his warrant card, he showed it to the woman. "I beg to differ," he stated. "We're with the Surrey Police, can you get him, please?"

The woman frowned at the ID, and then up at Jon. She grunted and looked annoyed. "Vas?!" she called out.

Jon looked over at Kate and smiled. "It's all in how you ask."

"Your social skills continue to amaze me," Kate replied.

"I bet they do! They are quite astounding, I know."

Kate rolled her eyes as they waited.

Meanwhile, inside, the woman called out a couple more times, eliciting an annoyed reply from deeper in the house. Before long, a man appeared sporting a buzz cut and wearing clothes that had seen better days.

"What is it, Yana?" he asked the woman, unhappy with being called to the door.

Yana nodded at the door. "Police."

Vassili looked up, his gaze cold and filled with daggers as he regarded them both. "What is it you want?" the man replied.

"Just to talk," Jon replied.

"I have no time to talk," Vassily replied.

"Well, I think you should make time, Vassili," John replied. "A girl that used to live here has gone missing, and I'd like to ask you about it."

"No girl from here has gone missing, as you say," the man answered. "Girl here, look," Vassili replied and pointed to Yana who'd answered the door. "No missing girl."

"What about Jacob?" Jon replied quickly.

"He is not here."

"So you know him? Oh good," Jon replied with a grin.

"Er…" Vassili replied.

"May we come in and talk to him?"

"No, you may not. There is no one here for you to talk to. No girl, no Jacob. Now, you go."

"This would be much easier if you'd just allow us to come in and make sure what you're saying is true."

"No. You go. You no come in," Vassily replied and pushed the door against Jon's foot. "Goodbye."

Jon relented and moved his foot. If the house's owner didn't want them to come in, and the grounds for entry into the property were sketchy at best, he thought it best to relent, and see where the other aspects of the case took them first.

"Well, they were friendly," Kate remarked as they walked back down the driveway, threading their way through several cars parked up there.

"I'd love to get in there," Jon replied.

"I know what you mean, but I'm not sure we have good enough grounds for that, yet."

"Nope."

"Shall we get a warrant? The chief will back us up."

"Perhaps, let's see where this goes first. Everything we have is speculation, and it's not the first time Olivia has disappeared, only to turn up later. So, I'd quite like to go and speak to Olivia's parents, see if they know anything, and try to get a little more out of Lily too. We can always come back here."

"Sounds like a plan."

10

"So tell me a little more about this case you had up north, with the Russians?" Kate asked as they drove north towards Croydon. "You mentioned it involved some trafficking?"

"That was part of it, but that's not how we got involved," Jon replied, thinking back. It had been one of those times when his personal vendetta against a killer got him in trouble with his superiors. But he couldn't see what he could have done better. He'd had to act. If he hadn't, a young woman would have been killed, and she wouldn't have been the last.

"It began with a tip-off about a businessman laundering money. So, we looked into it, and we discovered a river of money running through his company. But it wasn't clear where it was coming from exactly. So we started long-term surveillance on this guy. Fletcher Hughes was his name."

"Never heard of him," Kate admitted.

"No reason you should have. He was a wealthy man with an enviable family life who got in way over his head with these mob guys. He was living the high life and having a whale of a time. You know, drugs, girls, the usual."

"Oh, I see. A wife and kids weren't enough for him, then?"

"Apparently not," Jon replied.

"What is it with these people? They get a little bit of money and power, and it just goes straight to their heads. I've seen it a few times now."

Jon nodded, agreeing with her. He'd seen the same thing too and felt just as bewildered by the depths some people would sink to for money and power. The thing was, these things usually came back to haunt them, and they just got deeper and deeper into trouble, until someone like himself came knocking on their door.

"Well, it got worse for him," Jon continued. "It seems he was into some kinky stuff because he ended up killing one of the girls he was sleeping with."

"Who were these girls?"

"Russians mainly. Vulnerable girls who ended up in deep with the Mob. They were brought over to the UK and used by criminals to bribe people, get targets into compromising positions, that kind of thing. For Hughes, they were his reward for washing their money."

"And then he killed one?" Kate asked.

"Aye. Strangled her. We didn't know this until after the case had wrapped up, of course, but the Bratva bailed him out. They got rid of the body, putting him in even more debt to them."

"Nasty," Kate replied. "You called them Bratva?"

"It means 'Brotherhood', one of the names they use for themselves."

"These guys don't sound like people you want to owe."

"No, indeed. Anyway, turns out, after he'd done it once, Hughes got a taste for it. The Mob, of course, was only too pleased to provide for him as long as he kept his end of the deal."

"So, he laundered the Mob's money in return for them giving him girls to kill?"

"I know, it's sick. But we had no idea. We suspected something was up, but we were mainly looking into his financial crimes. Anyway, inevitably, someone found out. A woman discovered what Hughes was really doing, and threatened him with exposure. Furious, he told the Mob, who go after the threat. The woman came to me, scared, only for the Bratva to find and kidnap her. I managed to track her down, and find Hughes trying to kill her."

"I'm guessing you stopped it?"

"Of course, and in the process, ruined months of surveillance into the Mob's operations in the midlands. I only kept my job because I saved one, maybe two lives, and ended the reign of a vicious killer."

"Your mission," Kate muttered, nodding. He'd explained to her about his personal vendetta to hunt down and stop the worst killers in the UK.

"I told you I pissed off some of my superiors," Jon replied. "They weren't happy with me after that."

"You couldn't have handled it in any other way, though," she replied.

"Hell no. I wasn't going to walk away from someone in need," he replied, thinking back to the case, and still feeling troubled about it.

"I think you did the right thing," she replied. She tapped his knee with her hand.

He smiled, but it was an unconvincing one and replicated his own troubling memories of that case. "I did what I had to," he agreed as they drove into South Croydon and eventually found the street where Olivia's parents lived.

They were well away from the wealthy areas and soon found the modest boxy house that the Cooks called home.

"Do you think she's here?" Kate asked as they parked up and got out.

"No," Jon replied. "If she hated her parents enough to run away and stay away, I don't see why she'd come back."

"Yeah, I agree," Kate said, nodding as they wandered up the modest flagstone path and knocked on the door. It was answered a short time later by a woman who was perhaps in her fifties, with worry lines marking her face. She looked down at Jon with a world-weary expression, apparently singularly unimpressed with either of them.

"Yeah?" she asked.

"Mrs Sylvie Cook?" he began.

"Who's asking?"

"I'm Detective Jon Pilgrim, and this is DS Kate—"

"What do you want?" she cut in.

"Just a few minutes of your time, if that's okay? May we come in?"

Sylvie sighed a long, heavy sigh, as if this was the biggest inconvenience she'd ever encountered, and then rolled her eyes. "Alright, sure, come in," she replied and moved inside.

Jon followed Kate into a house that was quite untidy. Shoes lay scattered beyond the door and the mud they'd trekked in had been trodden into the old, stained carpet in the hallway. Beside a pile of letters, a couple of old carrier bags stood against the wall, filled with who knew what, while coats, gloves, and even a set of keys lay discarded.

Jon briefly considered asking if he should remove his shoes, and then guessed that it wouldn't make much difference to the carpet if he did walk some mud in, and just followed the woman inside.

She'd already taken a seat in the front room when he got there. She used the remote to put the daytime TV program on mute before she sat back, and gave him another long, annoyed sigh.

"What's she done this time?" Sylvie asked. "She's nothing but trouble, that one."

"Olivia?" Jon asked as he took a seat beside Kate.

Sylvie gave him a look, her eyes looking away briefly. "Err, yeah," she said, sounding like she was talking to a child. "That's who you're here to talk to me about, isn't it?"

Jon frowned, bristling at her attitude.

"Yes," Kate replied, her voice sweetness and light. "Have you seen her recently?"

"Nope," Sylvie answered, apparently unconcerned. "I've not heard from her in months. Why, should I have?"

"A friend of hers she was living with has reported her missing," Kate replied.

"So what else is new?"

"We suspect some criminality, maybe some abuse?"

"And I should care, because?"

Jon went to answer, but Kate cut him off. Good thing too, he guessed, given how he would have spoken to her.

"Because she's your daughter?" Kate replied, her voice calm and even.

The woman rolled her eyes and sighed again. "I gave up worrying about her a long time ago," Sylvie replied. "She's been nothing but a pain in my arse for years now, so as far as I'm concerned, good riddance to her."

"Even if she's been kidnapped?"

"I..." For a brief moment, her mask cracked, and a hint of emotion flashed across her face. She reined it in quickly though and took a moment to bring herself under control.

Jon eyed her, spotting this momentary lapse in her self-control, and wondered if he'd judged her wrong. She wasn't as uncaring as she made out, perhaps just the opposite. But it seemed to be something she kept hidden.

"Look, I don't want her to get hurt, but she's caused this family enough pain over the years. We can't take it anymore. I can't live my life waiting for her to come back to us. All I can say, is that she's not been back here in months. I've not seen her in ages, but if she does show up, I can let you know. Okay?"

"That would be great," Kate replied.

"Is your husband home?" Jon asked.

"No, Geoff's at work. He'll be back later on this afternoon though. Do you need to talk to him?"

It was Jon's turn to sigh. "We should touch base, at least."

"Fair enough. There was one thing though. One of Olivia's friends came by here yesterday evening. She was looking for her too."

"Lily," Jon replied.

"That's her. Someone else Livy has led astray, no doubt," she muttered and slowly shook her head.

"So, you have no idea where she might go?" Jon pressed.

"Nah," Sylvie answered. "Sorry."

"Or do you know anyone who might want to hurt her?"

She shrugged. "I don't know anyone in her life, and nor do I care to."

Jon found himself beginning to feel quite sorry for her. She looked broken, like someone who'd been dragged through the last few years by her daughter, showing the scars of caring for someone who didn't return those feelings.

She said she didn't care. She said she'd moved on, but Jon could see the lie of that now. It was a lie she'd probably told herself a million times in order to just get through the day, in order to function.

She could say she didn't care until she was blue in the face, but Jon felt sure he knew different. That brief show of emotion was enough for him to know that deep down, she did care for her daughter. She probably longed for her on a deep, primal level, but had done her best to cut herself off from that pain.

What was left, sat opposite them. A cold husk of a woman, waiting to allow herself to feel again.

He wondered if they'd be able to find Olivia and bring her back to her parents.

He hoped so.

"Thank you for your time," Kate said, finishing up the interview. "We will keep you informed of anything we discover, and let you know if we find her, okay?"

"Sure," Sylvie answered, and showed them out after they'd left their details behind should she remember anything, or if Olivia should show up.

"That is one broken parent," Kate commented as they sat in the car.

"I was thinking the same thing," Jon replied.

11

"So, how'd it go?" Nathan asked. "I can't imagine Vassili being very forthcoming."

"Aye, he wasn't. He really didn't want to speak to us. We didn't get in the house at all."

"We met him, and a girl called Yana," Kate added.

"Lily mentioned her," Jon remarked.

"Sounded like she was one of Jacob's friends," Kate said. "I can't imagine how another woman would want to be a party to abuse like that though."

"Money and power," Nathan replied as they walked through the office. "Money and power. Right, well, I figured this was starting to develop into something, so I set up an incident room."

"Good job," Jon replied, and followed Nathan through to the side room, complete with a meeting table and a large whiteboard with a photo of Olivia pinned to it.

Jon walked over to it and scanned the items that were pinned up. "Where did you get these from?" Jon asked.

"Dion got them from her Google photo account."

"That lad will go far," Jon remarked. There were pictures of Lily alongside Olivia, but nothing of Jacob, Vassili, or Yana. Olivia was a good-looking girl, with a striking face framed with dyed blonde hair and sapphire eyes that sparkled with life as she smiled for the camera.

Jon shook his head, finding the contrast between these happier times, and the dire straits Olivia possibly found herself in, troubling.

"She's a looker," Jon commented, nodding to Olivia's picture.

"That's probably one reason why Jacob targeted her," Kate replied. "If they were trafficking her, I'd guess that looks count for a lot."

"Makes sense," Jon answered.

"So what do you want to do with this Vassili?" Nathan asked.

"Right now, I'm not sure," Jon replied and chewed on his lip for a moment. "Let's get the team in and go through this," he said, and within moments, they were all sitting in the room around the table.

"So the visit to Vassili wasn't terribly productive. We know he's a criminal from his record, and there's nothing to suggest he's gone straight. In fact, if Lily is right, at the very least, he's letting abuse happen under his roof, possibly with his knowledge, or even encouragement. But he didn't let us in, so I have no idea who else, apart from Vassili and Yana, is in that house. Do we have any update on Jacob, or where he might be?"

"Nothing, no," Rachel replied. "We don't have a phone number for him or anything."

"He's probably using burner phones," Kate suggested.

Jon nodded. "Most likely. He's also our number one suspect, so we need to find him, and the most likely place for that is Vassili's house."

"So, we need a warrant," Nathan replied.

Jon nodded. "I think so. In the meantime, can we get a car outside Vassili's house? I want to know who comes in and who goes out, especially if Jacob turns up."

"I'll get that sorted," Dion replied, making a note.

"Good, thank you."

"Who's this Yana?" Rachel asked.

"I don't know," Jon replied. "She seemed like she was working with or for Vassili, and she had a Russian accent too."

"Do you think she's with the Mob?"

Jon shrugged. "Anything's possible."

"Money and power," Kate muttered.

"Aye," Jon replied.

Dion raised his hand.

"This isn't a school classroom, Dion," Jon said.

Dion drew back his hand, with a look of embarrassment.

"Don't scare the lad," Nathan commented to Jon, before looking over at Dion. "Don't let the big northern gorilla intimidate you, alright?"

"Word to the wise," Kate added. "Chips and gravy tend to calm him down."

"Gravy? On chips?" Nathan asked, scandalised. "That's wrong on like, so many levels."

"It's wrong on all the levels," Rachel added. "Probably on some levels we don't even know about."

"Surely that just turns them into a sloppy mess?" Nathan asked.

"Guys, guys. While I'd love to share this ambrosia of the gods with you sometime," Jon replied, raising his hands, "I'm going to have to insist that my demonstration of northern superiority waits for another day, okay? Now, Dion, you had something to say?"

"Um, yeah. I might have something that could throw a spanner in the works."

"Of course, you do," Jon replied. "It's been a spanner filled day, so one more might as well join in the fun."

"So, Lily said that Jacob got angry with her and Olivia after they went to that club, right?"

"That's right. They went off without him, and he was pissed at them for it."

"Okay, but what if it wasn't them just going to a club that annoyed him?"

"What are you getting at?" Jon asked, curious.

"I've been going through Lily's Google account, and I found some photos from that night," Dion said and handed out copies of a photo. Jon picked one up and saw Lily gurning at the camera, the slightly out of focus club behind her in the grainy image.

"What am I looking for?" Jon asked.

"In the background, that's Olivia, right?"

Taking a closer look, Jon could make out Olivia sitting amongst a bunch of other people, a drink in hand, smiling and enjoying herself. The background was slightly out of focus, but not by much, and he could clearly make out the faces of the people around her.

"She seems to be talking to that guy beside her," Jon remarked.

"Oh, I know him," Nathan said. "That's Russell Hodges."

"Wonderful, I'm pleased for you, I really am, but throw me a bone here. Who's Russell Hodges, and why the hell is he in my investigation?"

"He's a very wealthy local businessman," Nathan answered.

"I see," Jon replied, and looked at him again. "So, a standard Surrey resident, then. And how do you know him?"

"He was a suspect in one of my cases several years ago, back when I was still a DCI," Nathan replied, a troubled look drawing his eyebrows together. "He had a solid alibi though, and was backed up by others. We ended up arresting another man in the end. A guy called Alan."

"Okay, so Olivia met a wealthy local figure during a night at a club. Why do you think this is a spanner?" He addressed Dion.

"What if Jacob wasn't annoyed that Olivia went to a club, what if he saw this picture and got jealous?"

"I suppose that's possible," Jon mused. "Lily said that she hid her phone from Jacob, though."

"But what if he knew about it? It would make for a good way for him to keep tabs on her," Dion suggested.

"Hmm. So, he saw this photo and got angry. Makes sense," Jon replied and took another look at Olivia in the image. The man she sat beside was laughing along with her, and they were obviously being friendly. But was it anything more than that? Photos could be deceiving, but that was the point, he supposed. Maybe Jacob saw something that was, in reality, totally innocent? "Do you think this was anything more than just a friendly drink, though?"

"I know one person who might be able to shed some light on it, and she's downstairs," Kate said.

***

Jon placed the photo on the table in front of Lily and pointed to Olivia and Russell in the background. "What can you tell me about this?" Jon asked.

Lily leaned in and took a long look at the photo, and then looked up. He could see the worry in her eyes.

"It's okay," Kate said from where she stood behind Jon.

"We'd just like to know what happened between them," Nathan added, who'd also joined them.

"Are you okay?" Evie asked from nearby.

Lily nodded to her. "I'm fine, I want to help."

"So what do you remember?" Evie asked.

"Um, well, I'd forgotten about that. Olivia got talking to him and he was friendly back. But, they just talked," Lily replied, glancing up at them, and at her parents.

"That's all?" Jon pressed.

"Yeah, we got talking to them and joined their group. We just hung out, you know?"

"With Russell Hodges?" Jon said, pointing to the man beside Olivia.

"I guess," Lily replied, frowning at the image. "Yeah, I think that's what Olivia said his name was. She was all impressed by him, like. She seemed quite taken by him."

"Taken?"

"She was talking about him afterwards, about how well they got on and stuff. So, who is he?"

"He's a multimillionaire businessman," Nathan replied, his tone flat.

Lily looked up and blinked. "Oh…"

"Yeah," Jon replied. "Can you see why we're interested?"

"Yeah… In fact…"

"What?" Jon replied.

"I just wonder, because… Well, I don't know for sure. She was all cagy about it, but she said a few times that she was going to meet someone. She seemed really excited about it all."

"You mean, you think she was going to meet Russell?"

"I dunno. Maybe?"

"Okay, good, thank you, Lily. I understand you're heading home now, right?"

She nodded.

"We are," Nina, Lily's mother replied.

"As soon as you're happy for us to go," her father added.

Jon nodded. "I think you can go, as far as we're concerned. I'll leave the details up to Evie, but we might need to talk to you again soon, so stay in the area."

"We will," Nina replied.

"Thanks, and if you think of anything else, Lily, please get in touch, okay?"

"I will, and thank you," Lily replied before Jon led his team from the room and headed back upstairs.

"I want to talk to Russell," Jon said as they walked back into the office. "Even if he had nothing to do with this, he was one of the last people to see her before she went missing, and was possibly the catalyst for it too."

"I'll see what I can arrange," Kate replied and walked over to her desk.

Jon watched her go, and then looked up at Nathan, who seemed deep in thought. "What are you thinking?"

"I don't know, I've just... I've got an idea."

"What kind of idea?"

"It's probably nothing. Most likely a wild goose chase, so I'd rather not say, but... I'm going to look into something. I'll let you know if it works out though."

"Suitably mysterious, Fox. Alright, sure. You've intrigued me. Go ahead."

"Thanks, Loxley," he replied and walked off.

12

"So, have you met this Russell before?" Jon asked as they sped through the Surrey countryside, heading east towards Kingswood.

"No, but I know the case that Nathan is talking about, and frankly, he sounds like a prick."

"No, please. Don't mince your words, Kate. I want you to be honest with me, and tell me what you really thought of him."

"Har-di-har," Kate replied, giving him side-eye. "It was the Debby Steed case. Do you remember Debby Steed?"

"Yeah, the name rings a bell, where have I heard that before?"

"She was a TV personality. She fronted a 'cowboy business' show, exposing people running dodgy businesses."

"Oh yes, that's right. She was murdered, wasn't she?"

"Yep. They pinned it on the guy Nathan mentioned, Alan, but he always denied it. He said he was with Russell at the time of the murder, and then changed his story to Russell was the one who killed her. But Nothing ever stuck and Alan went down after several people spoke out against him, including Russell."

"I see. And Nathan ran that case, did he?"

"He did, it was one of the incidents that culminated in his demotion."

"How?"

"He was convinced that Russell, Alan, and others were part of some secret group. He saw conspiracy and ended up doing a one-man house invasion of Russell's property. He said he saw some kind of gathering there and called it in, but nothing was found, and although Russell didn't press charges against Nathan, he did get demoted."

"Because of Russell?"

"Nathan thinks so. Russell is close to several of the Police top brass, so…"

"I get it. The right word in someone's ear…"

"…and Nathan gets demoted," Kate added.

"You're right, he sounds like a prick."

"Told you." Kate laughed and then pointed. "Here we are."

Jon pulled into the driveway and up to the gate, pressing the button on the intercom. Several moments later, the speaker came to life. "Hello?"

"Hi, Detectives Pilgrim and O'Connell here to see Russell Hodges."

"Ah yes. Welcome, Detectives. Please, drive on through, and someone will meet you."

"Thank you," Jon replied, marvelling at the voice's plummy accent. "Oooh, lar-di-dar," Jon mimicked, once his window was up.

"We don't all talk like that," Kate replied.

"Well no, you're Irish, eh lassie?" he ended his sentence with an approximation of an Irish accent. It wasn't good.

"Well," Kate said, blinking as they drove into the property. "You butchered that one. I think a leprechaun somewhere just died."

Proceeding up the driveway, the mansion soon came into view, and it was one of the most impressive ones he'd seen yet. The place was huge, and sprawling, with several outbuildings surrounded by manicured lawns, bushes, and trees.

"Oh, wow. Now that is impressive. Mr Hodges has done well for himself.

"No shit."

A man walked towards their car as they parked up, although calling him a man was underselling him a bit, really. He could probably be more accurately described as a mountain, or a bull, or something else massive and dangerous looking.

Climbing out, Jon turned to meet the figure, confident that he was probably involved in Russell's security, somehow.

"Good afternoon, Detectives," the man said. "I'm Blake, Mr Hodges's head of security. I'll show you through to Mr Hodges. If you'd like to follow me?"

"Of course," Jon replied, and fell into step behind him, mentally checking off a point for his correct guess about this man's position.

Kate moved in beside Jon and gave him a look.

Jon wiggled his eyebrows in return as they approached an outbuilding that was long and squat, complete with a few garage doors along one side.

"It's a lovely place Mr Hodges has here," Kate remarked.

"He's worked hard to get where he is today, Miss O'Connell," Blake replied.

"Is he not in the house?" she asked.

"No, he's in the garage, I believe."

Jon wondered if they might actually see some of this guy's car collection, only to be proved right as they walked through a side door, to find an immaculate display of cars lined up along the left wall

There were McLarens, Aston Martins, Ferraris, and even a Lamborghini. Several cars in, two men stood talking. One was in a pair of overalls, but the other wore trousers and a shirt that looked they were worth more than Jon's monthly salary.

This was Russell. Jon recognised him from the photo, and he was having a friendly conversation with what Jon assumed was a mechanic.

As they approached, Russell noticed them, finished his conversation, and turned to greet them.

"Well, it's not often I get to welcome the Surrey Police into my home. Welcome, welcome..." he said, and then eyed Kate curiously. "I don't believe I've ever had the pleasure, Miss?"

"I'm DS Kate O'Connell, and this is DCI Jon Pilgrim. We'd like to ask you a few questions, if that's okay?"

"Of course. Please, come in. We'll head into the house and get a drink," he continued, focusing on Kate, almost to the exclusion of Jon. Russell quickly dismissed Blake as he ushered Kate along the line of cars.

Kate glanced back and winked without Russell noticing. Jon rolled his eyes and followed along behind them as Russell continued to chat.

"As you can see, I have some true classics in here. They're my pride and joy, and I love taking them out for a pootle along the local roads. They're beautiful, don't you think?"

"Oh yes," Kate replied, playing along. Jon couldn't help but take a moment to admire some of the vehicles on display, and allowed himself to lag behind a little as Russell continued ahead, regaling Kate with tales of his collection and how he acquired them.

Jon wasn't really much of a gear-head, but he could certainly appreciate some of the finer things in life, especially a nice car, such as some of the ones on display here.

He spotted a stunning polished Mustang, and with a glance at Kate moving up the building towards the far end, decided to indulge himself and have a closer look. He'd be quick, he had a job to do after all, but he just wanted to have a look inside. Moving around it, he found the interior was as gleaming as the paintwork. Walking back towards the front of the vehicle, he admired the front grille for a moment and the machine's beautiful lines.

"It's a work of art, isn't it?"

Jon straightened and turned to see a woman walking up to him. She was all curvaceous hips and dusky eyes, and her smile held unspoken promises, which made him feel uncomfortable.

"Um yes, it is. It's lovely," he replied, feeling a little uncomfortable under her gaze as she approached. He cleared his throat and tried to get his head back in the game. "I'm DCI Jon Pilgrim."

"I know."

"Oh, you know?"

"I saw you on the news yesterday, after that hostage case. That was some good work."

"Thank you, Miss, erm…"

"Sydney, Sydney Willow. I'm Russell's partner." She offered her hand.

Jon took it. "Nice to meet you."

"Likewise, Detective. I like a man with strong hands."

"Thanks." He wasn't sure how else to answer that.

"You like your muscle cars then? This is a classic American car, the Eleanor from that film, *Gone in 60 Seconds*. It truly is a beauty."

"It's gorgeous," Jon agreed.

"Expensive, too."

"I bet."

"I doubt you'd be able to afford such a vehicle on a DCI salary."

"Probably not," Jon agreed. His Astra was expensive enough for him right now, anyway."

"Shame."

"I suppose. So, you're Russell's girlfriend?"

She nodded, stepped up to him, and threaded her arm through his as she urged him to walk with her towards where Russell was regaling Kate.

"That I am. We've not been together long, though, so it's early days. It's been a bit of a whirlwind romance, I guess you could say," she answered, her voice whimsical as her heels clicked on the concrete floor. "Who knows? Maybe a big strong detective like yourself will come along and sweep me off my feet," she said.

Jon glanced over in surprise. She winked at him and bumped her hip into his, making him blush. He spotted Kate look his way and raise an incredulous eyebrow at him as he approached arm in arm with Sydney.

He mouthed the word 'help' at her, and she smirked, stifling a laugh.

"I see you've met my partner, Sydney," Russell said. He walked over, and pulled her in for a kiss.

"Where were you hiding, then?" he asked her with a smile.

"Oh, nowhere," she replied. "I was just introducing myself to Detective Pilgrim here." She looked up at Jon. "Are you going to introduce me to your partner?"

Jon stared at Sydney for a moment longer, trying to weigh her up. "Um, of course," Jon replied. "This is DS Kate O'Connell."

"A pleasure," Sydney said and offered her hand. She had a dark, dangerous look to her, and with her black hair, black outfit, and red belt, Jon found himself reminded of a Black Widow spider.

Pulling his eyes away, he silently admonished himself for those thoughts, feeling the presence of Kate, and the eyes of Charlotte in his head watching him.

Sydney smiled and glanced at Jon as she pulled away from greeting Kate. Jon caught her mischievous expression and felt a keen sinking feeling open up deep inside of him.

13

"Come in, come in," Russell said as they walked into a living room that was about the size of an average house, and could probably fit Kate's flat inside it several times over. Large paintings hung on the wall, and a white grand piano sat in the corner. In the centre of the room, a sunken area contained several comfortable-looking seats and sofas around a gilded coffee table.

Russell ambled through the room towards the seating area, taking his time. He seemed to enjoy showing off his wealth.

"Welcome to my humble abode. Please, take a seat, relax," he said, and then turned and addressed a woman who stood by one of the doors. "Ida, teas and coffees, please."

"Right away, sir," she replied and disappeared.

"Please, sit," Sydney said, gesturing to the sofas.

"Thank you," Kate answered, and moved to a sofa. Jon took a seat beside her on some of the nicest furniture he'd ever had the pleasure of sitting on Clearly, only the best would do for Russell.

Standing opposite them, he was all smiles and swagger. "So then, Miss O'Connell." Russell gave her a look. "It is miss, isn't it?"

"I'm pleased you're so relaxed and taking an interest in me," Kate began, "but that's not really an appropriate question."

Good, Jon thought, she wasn't falling for his easy charm and was keeping her eyes on the job at hand. He glanced over at Sydney as she took the seat next to him, crossing her legs and flashing him some thigh.

Jon pulled his eyes away.

"I'm sorry," Russell continued. "I just didn't want to insult you. I mean, you and Detective Pilgrim here might be an item for all I know."

Jon glanced over at Kate, surprised by Russell's comment. Kate frowned briefly, glancing back at him.

Russell smiled. "How's Nathan?"

"Nathan?" Kate asked, a clear note of surprise in her voice.

"He works with you, doesn't he?"

"Yeah," Kate answered.

"Sorry, as you can see, I do my research."

"We can see that," Jon replied.

"It was a shame what happened to him," he said. "Demoted when he had such a promising career ahead of him. Such a shame."

"We're not here to discuss that," Jon cut in. Was he goading them? It seemed like a provocative thing to say.

"I'm sorry, Detective Pilgrim. I didn't mean to derail the interview, I just have something of a history with Nathan and his 'theories,'" he said, raising his hands and curling his forefingers when he said that last word. "Aaah, here come the drinks."

Ida returned with a large tray with a pot of tea and a cafetière of coffee, surrounded by mugs, milk, sugar, and a plate of biscuits.

She made sure everyone had what they wanted, before leaving them to their conversation.

"Now, please, how can I help?" Russell asked.

"We were wondering where you were on Saturday night," Jon replied.

"Saturday? The seventh, right?"

Jon nodded, feeling very aware of Sydney's gaze boring into the side of his head.

"Well, I would have been out, but we went to a few places."

"How about Dance Fever in Epsom, did you go there?"

"We ended up there I think, yes. In the VIP room."

"Of course," Jon replied, knowing it was the room in the club that you could hire out and use privately.

Russell smiled at the comment. "Only the best, my man."

Jon grimaced, disliking his familiarity.

"Do *you* go clubbing much?" Sydney asked. Jon looked over to find her eyes fixed on him. "You should join us, sometime. You'd have a great night with us."

"Wonderful idea, Syd. Yes, you should," Russell urged.

"I'll pass, thank you," Jon answered, flustered by Sydney's attention. "So, going back to the night in question, do you remember this person?"

Jon placed a photo of Olivia on the table beside the tray and watched Russell's face with interest. He frowned slightly as he looked at the image. "Um, no, should I? I meet a lot of people, so it does tend to all blend together."

Jon pulled out a cropped, zoomed-in version of Lily's selfie that focused in on Russell and Olivia. "She was with you that night, in Dance Fever, and you seem to be enjoying her company in this photo."

"Oh, yeah, I think I remember a blonde. Yeah. That could be her," he added, pointing to the headshot of Olivia.

"It is her, I can assure you."

"I spoke with a lot of people that night, Detective."

"I'm sure you did."

"What is this about?"

"Olivia went missing two nights ago, and it seems that she was going to meet someone when she was taken."

"And you think that person was me?"

"We're just trying to ascertain what happened to her."

"I didn't arrange to meet her." He sounded offended. "I barely remember her and would have little desire to meet up with someone like that. How old is she? She looks really young."

"Sixteen," Kate replied.

"Then she shouldn't have been in that club," Russell answered.

"No, she shouldn't," Kate continued. "Do you regularly hang out with sixteen-year-olds, Mr Hodges?"

"No, but talking to them isn't a crime, is it? And I don't think I like where this conversation is going."

"We're just trying to get to the truth," Jon said.

"Well, I feel like I'm being interrogated and that you're insinuating things that are untrue." He looked furious and actually stood up as anger boiled up behind his eyes. Jon chanced a glance over at Sydney and found her looking up at Russell with a slightly amused look on her face that she hid when Russell looked her way.

"Please, Mr Hodges," Jon continued. "We're only trying to find a missing girl. That's all we want."

He nodded frantically. "I know. I know. I'm sorry. It just felt like you were accusing me of something."

"You were one of the last people to see and interact with Olivia, before she disappeared," Jon stated. "So it's important we talk to you. Did you notice anything strange about her? Did she seem worried about anything? Was she scared?"

"Honestly, I'd had a few to drink by then and my memory is a little hazy, but I don't think so, from what I can remember."

"So, nothing about her concerned you?"

"No, nothing. I think she was having a good time."

Jon sighed. There was little else for them here.

"Okay, thank you, Mr Hodges, I think that's all we have for you."

"My pleasure."

"One other thing," Kate cut in, and then looked over at Sydney. "Were you with Russell at the club that night?"

"No, sorry," Sydney answered. "I was here, waiting for him to get back."

"And can anyone corroborate that?"

"Only all the staff," she replied, with a smile.

Nodding, Kate turned back to Russell. "What about your security man, Blake, is it?"

"He was with me all night, he never leaves my side while we're out," Russell replied. "It's what I pay him for."

"May we speak to him?"

"Sure," Russell replied and called him in. Less than a minute later the man-mountain was standing by the table, looking down at the photos.

"Yeah, sure, I remember her," he replied. "She talked with Mr Hodges for a while, got him to buy her some drinks like they all do. They all just want his money, you know."

"I bet," Jon replied, and glanced at Sydney.

She gave him a brief smile in return.

"So, what happened, how long was she with you?"

"A couple of hours, then she and her friend disappeared. We didn't see them again," Blake replied.

"Thank you. Did she perhaps give either of you her phone number?"

"Half the ladies there were giving Mr Hodges their numbers," Blake replied.

"It's a curse," Russell said, having apparently regained his composure.

"Like I said, they're all after one thing," Blake added.

"So, Olivia gave you her number?"

"Possibly," Russell replied with a shrug. "I don't know. I always take them, but I always get rid of them too. I don't want to seem rude, but I have little desire to follow up on them."

"Of course you don't," Jon replied and glanced up at Blake. "Is that right?"

He nodded. "That's typical."

Jon returned the gesture and figured it would be a good idea to pull their phone records, and maybe have a look at the club's CCTV. He'd have to get Dion onto that once they were back.

"Okay, I think that's all," Jon said. "Thank you.

"Anytime," Russell replied.

"I'll see you out," Blake said.

"No, no," Sydney spoke up. "No need, I'll walk them out."

Blake didn't look terribly impressed with this and glared at her for a moment. It was only a brief look, but it wasn't the only time Jon had spotted an annoyed glance from Blake towards Sydney. He suspected there was little love lost in that relationship.

"Whatever," Blake replied after a beat.

Sydney smiled and ushered them out of the room, and through a corridor that was wider than most living rooms, to the front door.

"Thank you for coming, today, I hope you found what you wanted," she said. "It's a pleasure to meet you, Miss O'Connell, and you, Jon. Please, don't hesitate to come back if you have any other questions."

Kate nodded. "We will. Thank you for your help."

"Anytime. I'm only sorry we couldn't be more useful. I hope you find and save this missing girl." Sydney gave Jon a look during that last sentence.

"Me too," Jon agreed.

"I'm sure you'll find her soon. You're both excellent detectives, I can tell just from this meeting."

"Well, um… Thank you," Kate replied, and flashed Jon a glance, before she walked to the door and headed outside.

"See you soon," Sydney called after them. Jon fell into step beside Kate as they made their way back towards their waiting car in the fading light of the early evening.

Jon noticed how much of a piece of junk it seemed to be, sitting in these stunning grounds, and lamented the police's resources.

"*She* seemed to like you," Kate stated as they reached the car.

"Yeah, I noticed," Jon remarked. "I wonder what that's all about?"

"A distraction?" Kate suggested. "She was a stunning woman. You must have noticed?"

Jon gave Kate a look, sensing a trap in her words. "I wouldn't like to say."

"Because she distracted you?"

"Well, maybe a bit. But, it's not like I'd do anything."

"Of course you wouldn't," she replied, giving him a smile and a knowing look. "I'm messing with you, Loxley."

"Yes, you are. Stop it."

"Aye, aye, captain. But seriously, I'd be careful of her. She's trouble."

"You can say that again."

"She's trouble."

"You can say that again," Jon repeated again. Two can play at that game.

"Oh, piss off."

"Sorry," he replied, as they made their way back to the car and climbed in. "Want to go for a drink, tonight?"

Kate sighed. "Probably not, sorry. I'm tired and just need to get some sleep, really."

"Sure, I understand. But we're still on for Friday night?"

"Absolutely."

14

Sitting on the bed, with only a loose, old vest that hung from her shoulders and the thin, grubby sheets to protect herself from the cold in the room, Olivia felt helpless and abandoned.

She'd been right. There was only one reason she'd been brought here, and just thinking about it made her feel ill.

She looked over at her aching arm and the fresh needle marks where he'd pumped her full of more drugs to make her compliant. Blood had scabbed on her arm and dripped to the bed, adding yet another stain to the countless others.

How many girls had he brought here? How many had he abused? And what had he done with them once he'd become bored? She didn't like to think about that last one. She preferred to think that maybe one day, someone would come for her, find her, and free her from this nightmare before the worst happened.

Now, more than ever, she wanted to go home.

It wasn't something she'd ever really considered over the last year, until recently. She'd always hated her parents and how they'd treated her. But now she knew different.

Now she'd truly experienced pain, abuse, and hate. Her parents hadn't been abusive. They'd just wanted her to go to school, get an education, and make something of her life.

She saw the wisdom in that now, but it was too late. She should have come to that realisation a long time ago. Instead, she'd thought herself clever and grown-up for choosing her own path.

Her parents had never hit her, never hurt her.

Being sent to her room after a stern word seemed like a luxury now, it would be a paradise compared to what she'd been through.

Was this Jacob's place, she wondered?

Had he sent his friends for her? Had they found her in that car park and brought her here to take revenge?

God, she wished she could just go home. She wanted her mum. She wanted to see Lily and hug her close. Her friend didn't deserve the life she'd dragged her into.

Shame brought heat to her cheeks as she thought back to how she'd convinced Lily to come with her, to live with her and Jacob at his cool house. They could skip school and just have fun, drink, and enjoy the life Jacob offered them.

But that offer had been a lie, a trap, baited to lure them in with the promise of money, freedom, and whatever else they wanted.

She saw it plainly now, she saw it for what it truly was, and she hated herself for urging Lily to join her in that trap. She remembered the hateful things she'd done, how Jacob had poisoned her against her own parents, and how she'd then done the same to Lily, making her think they didn't want her around.

She should have brought Lily with her. She should have insisted. But she was still back there, with Jacob and Vassili.

"Oh Lily, I'm sorry," she muttered. "I hope you're okay."

As she sobbed into the sheet, ignoring the acrid stench that came from it, she heard footsteps from somewhere in the house. They were getting closer, and louder, coming up some steps. Her heart raced as her chest tightened with fear.

"No… Oh God no, not again."

15

Nathan emptied his pockets, placing his keys, phone, and change on the tray provided.

"You're in late, sir," the prison officer commented.

"Yeah, sorry," Nathan replied.

"It's no problem. We're getting him ready for you. If you'd like to follow George there, he'll take you through," the officer said, pointing up the corridor.

Nathan followed the man's gesture and walked up to the officer who nodded to him. "Evening, Detective. This is a late visit."

"Can't be helped, he could prove useful in an investigation," Nathan replied. "Has he had any visitors?"

"Just his wife, but no one else. He gets letters occasionally, but they're all banal stuff. Nothing useful."

"I see," Nathan replied, wondering what hidden messages there might be in these boring letters. Or was he being overly suspicious again? That was certainly possible. It was a habit that he tried to rein in whenever possible as it had a habit of alienating people.

The walk through the prison took several minutes as they navigated through several locked security doors until he was finally shown into a room with a table, a few chairs, and little else.

"Take a seat, he's on his way," George suggested.

Nathan nodded, choosing to remain standing for now, and paced up and down the room, wondering if this next conversation would confirm his theory.

Moments later, the door clanged open and Alan Peck walked in. With his hands cuffed, two prison officers guided him to a chair and urged him to sit.

"Nathan," Alan said sounding surprised, not yet taking a seat. "Well, this is a turn up for the books. I didn't expect to see you here. So, what's this all about? A social call? Are you writing your memoirs maybe? Hmm?"

"Sit," one of the officers barked at him.

Alan sighed, and dropped into the seat, rolling his eyes. Satisfied, the officers moved away. One of them stayed in the room by the door as security, which Alan took note of.

"It's all fun and games in here," Alan said. "So what can I do for you, Halliwell?"

"I came here because I have some questions for you."

"Questions? How spiffing. I do love a quiz. Go ahead, and make it a good one, Nathan."

"I want your opinion on someone."

"Jesus fucking Christ, Nathan, spit it out, will you? Who? Who do you want my clearly valuable opinion on?"

"Russell Hodges."

"Russell? I would have thought that would be fairly obvious. The guy is a cock."

"Because he testified against you, saying you killed Debby Steed?"

"You were on the case, Halliwell, you know how that went down. I did not kill her, despite what everyone else thinks."

"So tell me more about him," Nathan suggested. "Tell me about the kind of man he is."

Alan narrowed his eyes as he stared across the table at him. "Why? What's going on? Is he a suspect in another case?"

"I'm not at liberty to disclose any details, we just need to know a little more about the kind of things he gets up to."

Alan continued to stare across the table, a suspicious and troubled look writ large across his face.

"You're aware of who you're dealing with, right?" Alan asked.

"He's a wealthy man, yes."

"And connected. Very well connected."

"To who? To what?"

"To all the right people. The man has friends in high places, and these walls have ears. Besides, what on earth do you think you'll be able to do to him? Huh? Do you honestly think you'll be the one to take him down? Over what?"

"You tell me."

Alan sighed. "I wish I could. The man is an idiot, I make no bones of that, but as far as anything else, what would I know?"

"I think you know more than you're letting on."

"You can think what you like, it's a free country… so I'm told."

"Why are you protecting him?"

"Him? You think I'm protecting him? Hell no," Alan replied, and then leaned forward and whispered. "I'm protecting myself. If I'm good, keep my head down, then maybe one day I'll get out of here. I am not about to jeopardize that on the frankly paper-thin hope that you and your idiot friends will be able to take down one of the country's richest men. He's got lawyers up the wazoo."

"Sounds uncomfortable."

Alan shook his head.

"I think you know more than you're letting on, but you're scared of him."

"Fuck me, Sherlock's in the room, careful."

"I'm right, aren't I?"

"Of course I'm fucking scared of him, but if you think I'm going to tell you anything, you have another thing coming. Why would I trust you or the police after what I've been through? You failed me. The justice system failed me, and now my life's in tatters. Ruined, because of you and your shitty friends. So no, I don't trust you, and nor will I ever trust you."

"So you can't tell me anything?"

"I know these men well enough to know when you might as well give up. They're wealthy, powerful, and will get all up in your shit if you annoy them. There's nothing you can do against them."

"I think you're wrong," Nathan replied.

"Well, good luck with that."

"So, you have nothing you can tell me? You're going to let an innocent victim have their life ruined by the actions of these men?"

"Don't guilt-trip me, Nathan, you're not good at it."

"On your conscience be it."

Alan sighed. "Look, all I can say is, he has some... questionable friends."

"Like who?"

"You're going to have to work that out for yourself, Nathan. We're done here," he replied and stood. "Guard."

The guard by the door knocked on it, and his friend appeared, followed by George. The two guards moved to Alan's side. "Come on then."

"It's been a delight, Detective, truly it has. Give my regards to Kate, By the way, how's her finger?"

Nathan didn't answer the question, but he did look up and catch the smirk on Alan's lips as he was led out of the room.

George approached the desk that Nathan sat behind. "Did you get what you wanted?"

"Kind of," Nathan replied. "Kind of."

16

Pulling up in the hotel car park Jon turned the car off, plucked the foam food carton from the passenger seat, and sat back. Picking one of the lengths of garlic-sauce-covered kebab meat from the warm pitta bread, he stuffed it in his mouth and savoured the greasy taste. He didn't have one of these very often, but they were just so good, especially after a long day of policing and dealing with pricks like Russell.

What was the deal with him, and why did his girlfriend, Sydney, take such a keen interest in him? That was downright uncomfortable.

Maybe they were one of those couples? Swingers? Perhaps they held sex parties at that mansion and shared partners?

The thought was an intriguing one, but he wasn't sure. It was more likely that she was doing it on purpose, trying to seduce him for whatever reason. Was it at Russell's behest?

Jon munched on another mouthful of processed lamb and wondered how Russell might connect to Olivia and her disappearance. He'd met her at that club, they had definitive proof of that, but he seemed like he had no idea who she was. Had he been lying? Sydney had been right there, and might not have liked the idea of him picking up a teenager for a night of passion, so of course, he'd lie if he had actually done something with her.

He struck Jon as the kind of man who would play away, getting his end away whenever he could, mainly because of the attention he got from being in his admittedly enviable position.

The impression Jon had of him was of a used car salesman got lucky. Somehow, he'd become incredibly rich, but if Jon was right about him, he'd guess it was through underhanded means and methods. He'd probably swindled his way to the top. There was no way a man like that got his wealth through kosher business deals.

Or, maybe he was wrong.

But he doubted it.

Well, there was little point in sitting here in a dark car park. He might as well sit in a warm hotel room instead.

Jon climbed out of the car and walked in through the main entrance, pulling his room key out as he went.

"Hey, Pilgrim."

Jon turned at his name to see Kate sitting nearby in the hotel lobby, beaming up at him.

"Oh, hi.What are you doing here?"

"I changed my mind."

"About what?"

"About spending the evening with you. I thought it might be nice to get a drink in a more relaxed environment."

"Oh," he replied in surprise and then smiled. "Well, that sounds good. What did you have in mind?" he asked as she stood.

"I'm not talking about a wild night on the town, by the way."

"Good, because I've just had a kebab, and I doubt I could manage one anyway. So how about a hot drink in the hotel bar?"

She smiled. "Perfect."

"Great."

"So, a kebab?" she asked as they walked through. "Shish or doner?"

"Doner, with a generous covering of garlic sauce. Can't beat it."

"Sounds good," she replied without much enthusiasm. "Just don't get too close with that garlic breath of yours, okay?"

"No tonsil hockey, then?"

"In your dreams."

Jon nodded and smiled, but a part of him wondered how serious she was about that. Was she just messing with him, or was she telling him she only wanted to be friends?

"How about that table over there?"

"Looks good," Jon replied, and before long they were settled in their seats, and a waiter had taken an order of tea for them both.

"So, what do you think of my home?"

"Well, it's a little crowded for my tastes. I prefer to not share my dining room with the general public, but it's nice and big."

"Isn't it?" Jon replied proudly.

"Did you put an offer in on the house?"

"I did, actually. The seller sent back a counteroffer, and I need to get back to the agents with my reply. Looks like I'll be bargaining with them."

"Did you lowball it on your first offer?"

"A bit. Gotta save those pennies."

"I guess. I hope you get it, it was a nice place."

"Thanks," he replied, as the tea was brought to the table and they poured it out.

"Do you want me to do yours?" Kate asked, a mischievous grin on her face. "I can even use my tea making magic and put the milk in first."

"Stay away from my drink, witch," he replied, raising his hands and crossing his fingers to make a cross. "I'll have none of your alchemy infecting my tea."

She laughed. "So, you've been here a few weeks now, and I've not really seen you for most of it. How are you settling in? It's not too bad down south, is it?"

He laughed. "No. In all honesty, I like it, I do. There are some differences, sure. The price of things is crazy…"

"Like houses?"

"Like houses. I could buy a mansion up my way for what I'll be paying down here. But that's okay, it's just the way it is."

"So you don't miss home?"

"A bit. I have lots of memories up north, sure. But that's all, really."

"Any family?"

"Oh yeah. My parents still live in Mansfield, and my sister is up there too."

"You have a sister?"

"Yep. Jill."

"Jon and Jill? Inventive."

"I know, right? It's one step away from Jack and Jill."

"Went up the hill to fetch a pail of water…" Kate sang.

"Oi you, shut it. I've never fallen down a hill and broken my crown."

"Are you sure? I sometimes wonder," she replied with a wry smile.

"What about you? Any family local? You went to stay with your parents recently, right?"

"Yep. Just my mum and dad, I'm an only child. They live near Maidenhead. They lived in Sutton before that, but moved after my one woman excursion to Ireland."

"Maidenhead. That's near Windsor, right?"

"Closer to Slough, but yeah."

"Aaah, *The Office*, I loved that series."

Kate laughed. "Yeah. It's not as bleak in Slough as *The Office* made it out to be, though. I used to go out clubbing there."

"You dirty stop out. I bet you were tearing up the town."

"We had some fun times."

"Friends?"

"Of course, a bunch over Maidenhead way. One of my childhood friends lives locally in Leatherhead too. Harper. That's why I chose to get a flat there."

"Makes sense."

"Have you got any friends or relatives down here?" she asked.

"Nope. No one."

"Aww, how sad. I'll be your friend."

Jon snorted. "Thank you, Detective."

"Anytime." She smiled brightly.

"So, any idea what Nathan's up to?"

"No, why?"

"He's following some kind of lead on the case. No idea what, but I said he could look into it."

"Yeah. He can be a bit of an enigma, that one. He's great, I enjoy his company, but he plays his cards close to his chest. I felt like I never really fully got to know him. He's a great detective though, even if he does have some interesting ideas about the world."

"The conspiracy theories? Yeah, that was a little strange. It all seems to come from a distrust of the rich and powerful, I think."

"Yeah, I noticed that. Which sounds about right for this area where he's surrounded by it. You can't fling a stone for hitting a millionaire around here."

"I bet that only feeds his paranoia. That and dealing with criminals day in and day out."

"You're probably right," Kate agreed. "You worked with him while I was away, though, right? Did you get on okay with him?"

"Yeah, of course. I'm easy, I'll get along with anyone. He's alright, I don't have any complaints."

"And the rest of the team?"

"No, I like them all. I think I've fallen quite lucky. I've hung out with them at the pub a couple of times."

"See, you're making friends already. It looked like that Sydney was keen to be your friend too."

"I think she wanted more than that," Jon remarked. "I half expected her to turn up here and try something."

"But instead, you got me, the Tea Witch. Sorry."

"I'll make do."

Kate laughed.

17

Geoff awoke with a start, his eyes blinking in the darkness. Had he heard something?

No, he must be imagining things, surely. With a sigh, he closed his eyes.

There was another thud, followed by the sound of movement from somewhere in the house. Beside him, Sylvie stirred too. He sat up.

"Urgh, what's that noise?" she muttered, her voice low.

"Ssshh, quiet. I think someone's in the house."

"What?" she gasped. "You're kidding." He could see her eyes bug in the shadows as fear gripped her. He felt the same creeping terror in his chest, and part of him just wanted to hide under the covers and hope whoever it was, went away.

There was another thud, and Sylvie whimpered.

"Shush," he hissed.

But he couldn't just hide, he couldn't just do nothing. He had to do something, Sylvie was relying on him. There were more thuds, getting closer this time, and a reflected light swept over the walls through the doorway.

Torchlight.

Someone was coming upstairs.

Geoff balled his fists as his breath grew short. He could feel a swiftly growing anger boiling up inside of him at the audacity of whoever it was. How dare they come into this house, invade their personal space, and… and…

He didn't know why they were here. Were they going to try and rob them?

No. He wouldn't allow it.

Geoff climbed out of bed and inched towards the door. The light swept across the wall again.

Geoff jumped back.

"What are you doing?" Sylvie whispered.

"I don't know," he replied, furious, but still scared.

"Shut the door."

"What?"

"Shut it, and hold it closed. They can take whatever they want, I don't care."

"No, I won't let them."

"Don't go out there, please," she pleaded.

"I'm just going to scare them off."

"Geoff please, don't. I'll call the police."

There were more sounds of movement coming from the next room.

Olivia's room.

What were they…? A thought occurred to him, was it Olivia? Was she back? He looked at his wife.

"Is… is it her?" she asked, having the same thought. "Is my baby home?"

"I…" He needed to know. Geoff strode out of the room onto the dark landing and around to Olivia's room, peering into the darkness. "Livy? Is that you?"

A tall, dark figure appeared before him, stepping into the doorway of his daughter's room. It was not Olivia.

He gasped. "Huh… who are you? What do you want?"

The figure moved, too quick for him to follow in the darkness. Pain blossomed on his forehead.

"Aaagh," he cried before the man pushed him. He hit another figure behind him. Geoff tried to pull away but was hit again. He fell and saw a boot come rushing towards his head.

18

Jon walked across the office towards the incident room, his files under his arm as he did his best to get his head in the game.

He'd slept badly, and it was taking its toll on him today. He'd been preoccupied with the case, running through possibilities in his head about what this was leading to and where Olivia might be. The link to the Russian Mob through Vassili was worrying him too. He'd seen firsthand the kind of devastation they could wreak, and had no desire to see that kind of thing again.

And then there was Russell and Sydney.

He didn't trust either of them, but he felt like Sydney had taken something of a personal interest in him, and that just made him think back to Charlotte and the man who had taken her life, because of what he'd done.

As a result, his mind had been racing all night, leading to him tossing and turning in bed, and having a couple of vivid nightmares that he wouldn't wish on anyone.

"Hey, how was your night?" He looked up to see Kate approaching with a smile. "Are you okay?"

"Hi. Um yeah, I'm okay, thanks. Just a little preoccupied."

"I could tell when you walked in. You looked like you were miles away from here."

"Yeah," he agreed. "I just had a bad night's sleep, you know?"

"Don't lie."

"Huh?"

"I bet after I left, you went out and tore up the town, right? You dirty stop out." She smirked.

Jon laughed. "If only. Two pints and I'm anybody's these days."

"Two pints," she replied, pulling out an imaginary notebook and miming writing in it. "Noted."

"And by anybody's, I mean I usually end up embracing the floor, or calling God on the big white telephone."

"God on the what?"

Jon made a vomiting noise.

"Oh." She laughed as they walked into the incident room. "Thanks for the tea last night, by the way. It was good to catch up." She winked at him.

"I had fun too. I'm looking forward to Friday."

"Me too." She smiled and walked to her seat.

Jon took his seat and looked up at his team with a smile. "Morning, I hope you all got a better night's sleep than I did."

"Yup," Kate replied.

"Not too bad, guv," Dion added.

"Where's Fox?" Jon asked, noting Nathan's absence from the meeting.

"Don't know," Rachel replied.

"No idea," Kate added. "I've not seen him. His coat is on his chair out there, though."

"Hmm, okay. Maybe he'll turn up."

"He wasn't around much yesterday afternoon, either," Rachel said.

"Hmm. Well, he did say he was chasing up a lead."

"Any clue as to what?"

"Nope," Jon replied. "He was being all mysterious about it. I'll have a hunt around for him in a bit. Okay, let's focus on Olivia Cook, what do you have to tell me? Anything new? Has she turned up anywhere yet?"

"No, nothing yet, guv," Dion replied. "No new reports. Nothing."

"Alright, then we work the case. I still want into Vassili's house. Where's my warrant for that?"

"We should get it today," Rachel replied. "I've been digging a little deeper into Vassili, and it looks like we've dug up quite the career criminal. I've reached out to the police in Russia, but I'm not sure what we'll get back. I suspect he was a low-level criminal over there too, though. In fact, I think he might have been sent over here to extend the influence and power of the Mob family he works for."

"Good work, but that only confirms what I'd feared. The sooner we get into that house, the better. Let me know as soon as we have that warrant."

"Will do."

The door to the room opened, and Sheridan walked in with a sheepish grin on her face. "Sorry I'm late," she said and moved to her seat before greeting the others.

"Between downstairs and up here?"

"Yeah, well, there was a—"

"Whatever, better late than never," Jon interrupted and returned to his train of thought. "So, what about Jacob?"

"Still missing," Kate said. "We've got officers parked up close to Vassili's house, they've been there all night, but there's no sign of Jacob so far, and there's been nothing incriminating either."

"What're the chances of Vassili or Jacob knowing we're watching the house?" Jon asked, wondering if they'd been made already.

"It's certainly possible," Kate replied.

"Okay, well let's keep them there for now. They'll be a deterrent at least."

Kate nodded.

"We need to know more about Russell Hodges too," Jon said.

"You think he might be involved?" Kate asked.

"In the kidnapping? I honestly don't know, but I doubt it. Not directly at least anyway. I can't see him smuggling a girl into a vehicle in a car park, but I just wonder if there's something dodgy going on with him. I'd like to know if he has any links to any criminals or organised crime."

"Like the Russians?" Rachel asked, her eyebrows raised.

"Yeah, maybe. Stranger things have happened."

"On that point," Dion said. "I've put in a request for the CCTV from the club in Epsom, where Russell was photographed with Olivia. I'll go through it as soon as we get it. I've also requested Russell's phone records and those of his employees."

"Excellent," Jon replied. "If that's all?"

"There's one other thing I think you should know," Sheridan said, leaning forward.

"Aye, go on love," Jon replied, looking at the blonde CSM.

"You were just talking about Russell Hodges, right?"

"Yeah...?"

"Well, he's here."

"Here? As in, in this building?"

Sheridan nodded. "He's out there in the office, right now," she said, pointing out into the main SIU office. "The assistant chief constable is showing him around."

"What?" Jon replied astounded. "What on earth? How? Why?"

"I dunno," Sheridan said, putting her hands up in the air. "Don't shoot the messenger."

Jon went to answer, but couldn't find the words and just spluttered as he stood up and moved to the door. "I'll see what's going on," he said.

"I'll come with you," Kate said.

"I'm not missing this," Rachel added, and the rest followed her out.

Sure enough, at the far end of the main room, the assistant chief constable of the Surrey Police was standing in his black uniform beside Chief Superintendent Collins, Russell, Blake, and Sydney, showing off the office, like a proud father might his child.

Jon stopped in his tracks and found himself rooted to the spot at the sheer audacity of the pair of them.

"Shut your mouth, Jon, you'll start catching flies," Kate said in low tones.

"Wha... Oh. What the hell are they doing here? He's a bloody suspect, and this is an active case. Is the ACC insane?"

"He probably has no idea," Kate replied.

"Jesus fucking Christ, this is bollocksed up," Jon said spitting the words out.

"No shit," Kate replied.

"What's his name, the ACC?"

"Miles Ward," Rachel offered.

"That's right," Jon replied, remembering. "Nathan was talking about him."

"He doesn't like the man," Kate confirmed.

"Can't say I'm feeling charitable towards him right now either," Jon agreed.

"DCI Pilgrim," the chief called out, and waved him over. "Jon, come and join us."

"Oh, God." Jon gulped. "Here we go."

"Go get 'em, tiger," Kate stated.

"Grrr…" Jon muttered, and strode off across the office, taking a moment to affix as convincing a smile as he could to his face.

"Jon. This is Assistant Chief Constable Ward, he's just showing Mr Hodges here around. Hodges is a keen supporter of the police and has donated much to the force over the years. He was interested in this new unit, so as a friend of the Police, ACC Ward offered him a tour."

"Oh, did he now?" Jon replied, his tone flat. He could see that the chief was also not too happy about the situation, as his smile was anything but genuine and his voice sounded strained. ACC Ward didn't seem to notice though and nodded happily.

"Russell is a long-time friend of mine *and* the Surrey Police. He's a pillar of this community," Ward said, sounding proud to be stood beside Russell.

"I see," Jon answered, becoming keenly aware of how much this might complicate things for them going forward. His overwhelming feeling was that he desperately wanted a chasm to open up beneath him right now and swallow him whole. This was all kinds of fucked up.

"Have you met Russell's lovely partner, Sydney Willow?" Ward asked.

"I...um. I'm not sure I have."

Sydney offered her hand and smiled mischievously at him. "Charmed, I'm sure."

He shook it briefly. "Yeah, likewise," he replied, deadpan.

"So we took on DCI Pilgrim only recently," the chief said. "He came down from the Nottingham Police force after being recommended to us by Inspector Verner of the National Crime Agency."

"And he leads your team of officers as they take on these serious crimes?"

"That's correct," the chief replied and looked up at Jon, his eyes bugging for a second when no one was looking.

"So, SIU," Sydney asked, "what does that stand for?"

"The team's full acronym is SOS-SIU, which stands for Serious, Organised and Serial, Special Investigations Unit."

"That's a bit of a mouthful," she replied.

"We just go by SIU, most of the time," Jon replied. "Less of a mouthful."

"So, can we...?" Russell started, making to walk deeper into the room.

"I'm sorry, no. We have some delicate ongoing cases," Jon replied quickly, holding his arms up to block the way. "Authorised personnel only, I'm sure you understand."

The ACC looked immediately annoyed.

"Oh, of course," Russell answered. "I didn't mean to intrude."

Of course you didn't, Jon thought sarcastically and noticed that the ACC frowned at him briefly, and then looked between him and the chief.

"Do you not have a superintendent?" the ACC asked.

"No," the chief replied. "But we do okay as we are."

"Hmm, well, we can't have that," the ACC answered. "You need a full and proper chain of command in place. It's only right. In fact, I know just the person for you. I'll get one installed for you as soon as possible. Leave it with me."

"I think we'll need to run that by the NCA, as this is as much their unit as it is the Surrey Police's."

"I'm sure that will be no trouble," the ACC replied. "I'll talk to them. But that's even more reason to have everything present and correct. Your jurisdiction is quite sweeping, so we need to be sure we're doing things by the book."

Jon glanced at the chief and could see him bristling at this, possibly even more than Jon was. He could already guess the kind of person the ACC would bring in, and it did not bode well.

"Everything okay?" Kate said as she stepped up to the group. "Hi, I'm DS O'Connell."

"Kate is another of our valued officers," the chief added.

"Kate," Russell said in greeting. "It's such a pleasure to meet you. So you're on this SIU team then?"

Looking over, Jon caught a glance from her. He gave her a look back and hoped that she'd play along with this farce, and not give away that they'd actually just met yesterday. The ACC seemed unaware of this little fact, and would likely not enjoy being made to look like an idiot.

Which of course, he was, Jon thought. A great bloody idiot.

"Kate," Russell continued. "Why don't you come with us and help show us around. Give us a detective's point of view on things?"

"A great idea," the ACC agreed, apparently thrilled by Russell's suggestion.

"Off you go then," the chief said, and Jon could see the look of a deer trapped in headlights on her face as the ACC and Russell set off, guiding Kate to join them.

As they walked out of the SIU office. Kate glanced back, looking utterly terrified.

Jon could only shrug as Kate's eyes rolled before she accepted her fate, and went with it.

"Jesus," the chief cursed once they were out the doors.

"What the hell are they doing here?" Jon snapped. "We were interviewing them yesterday, as suspects in this bloody case."

"I know. They just turned up. The first thing I knew about it they were walking in the fucking door."

"This is messed up."

"Well done on keeping them from looking around the office," the chief said.

"Huh, yeah, looks like it'll cost us though. Ward didn't seem too happy about that."

"You insulted his stinking rich friend, I'm not surprised."

"This just gets better and better." Jon sighed. "Right, I've got someone I need to find."

"Oh?"

"Nathan's gone rogue on me."

"Oh, he does that. I think I heard he was in the basement, in the records room."

"Records room, great, thanks."

19

Jon made his way downstairs, rubbing his face at the display of hubris he'd just seen upstairs. He really didn't understand what was going through the ACC's head, thinking that it was a good idea to bring a civilian in here with no warning whatsoever.

He could see why Nathan wasn't a fan of his. He had his nose so far up Russell's arse that he'd lost all sense of proper police etiquette. But then, he guessed that was what money did to some people.

Jon made his way down to the basement level, which he'd visited before for the changing rooms that were down here. He'd never really fully explored it though, and hadn't been aware there was a records room until the chief mentioned it.

It wasn't too difficult to find, however, located at the end of the main basement corridor. Jon thanked his lucky stars that he hadn't bumped into the millionaire tour that was going on and pushed the door open into the records room beyond.

The room's size was quite surprising, taking up most of the station's footprint. It was filled with rows of metal shelving, stacked high with filing boxes that spread out from the shelves onto the floor and piled up along the walls. Jon noticed dehumidifiers mounted to the walls that hummed away in the background as he walked along one of the aisles, to an open area a short way in. Nathan stood beside a table, leaning over a file he was leafing through. Around him, boxes were open, and files lay discarded here and there. There was a laptop open on the table too, logged into the Police database.

"Morning, Nathan," Jon said as he stuffed his hands in his pockets and surveyed the scene.

"Is it?" Nathan replied without looking up.

"Losing track of time?"

"I've been busy."

"I can see that," Jon replied. "You're making a mess, too."

"I'll clean it up."

Jon nodded. "I had no idea all this was down here. I thought the station was a fairly recent build?"

"It is, but its modern facilities and space meant that some older storage rooms in stations around the county were cleared out, their files moved here so they could be better looked after."

"I'm getting some serious *Indiana Jones* vibes, looking at these stacks. Maybe the Holy Grail's in here, somewhere?"

"One can only hope." Nathan smirked, closed the file he was looking at, and dropped it to one side on the table.

"Nothing in that one?"

"Nope." He sighed. "Nothing I'm looking for."

"And, what are you looking for, Fox?"

Nathan sighed and slumped into a chair. "I… I might be chasing a ghost, I don't know, but I was sure that I heard of a case a while back that was linked to Russell."

"What kind of case?"

Nathan looked over, raising his eyebrows. "A missing girl."

"Oh, another one? So, this isn't the first of this kind of case?"

"Heh, well, I don't want to jump to any conclusions, and my memory isn't what it once was, but I was sure I'd heard of a case a year ago or so, that was similar to this one."

"Well, if you can find it, I'd love to see it, and it would certainly make the Russell angle more compelling if this has happened before."

"I know, that was my thought too. It just came to me when I heard Russell's name come up. It triggered a memory of something. I've done some hunting through the system, but Russell's name isn't linked to anything like that on there. I don't know, maybe I'm barking up the wrong tree here, but I needed to look into it."

"Isn't that a little odd, details not being on the system?"

"I guess. I've seen it happen before, though. Maybe not everything got logged by the officers on the case. Some of the older guys used to prefer working on paper and got others to enter the details."

"Hmm, or maybe there was pressure from above to keep the name off the system?"

Nathan pulled a face. "An interesting idea. What makes you think that?

"Russell's is in the building being shown around."

"What? How the hell?"

"Assistant Chief Constable Ward is here giving him a guided tour."

"Well, that's just wonderful, that is. Why don't we just invite all the criminals in and show them our case files? The bloody idiot, what does he think he's doing?"

"I don't think he was aware of our investigation into Russell."

"I'd hope not because if he was, then that's a thousand times worse."

"I know," Jon replied. "Maybe he'd also order us to back off, and maybe that's what happened before?"

"That's a hell of an accusation, Jon."

"I know. Let's play this close to our chest for now. I don't want the brass knowing about the Russell link."

"Will do. I'll keep looking. If there's a scribbled note in here with Russell's name on it, I'll find it."

Wandering around the table, Jon looked over the files and some of the photos that had spilt out of them. Images of people long dead, their lives snuffed out, ended before their prime. It wasn't a pleasant scene. "Tell me more about Russell. Kate filled me in about the Debby Steed case."

"I figured she might, given that he was involved."

"You suspected him, right?"

Nathan sighed. "The case around Alan Peck was flimsy, to be honest, and had Russell backed him up, he probably would be a free man right now, but Alan's defence seemed to revolve around Russell supporting his alibi. But he didn't. Instead, he denied that Alan had been with him."

"But you suspected something else, right?"

"You know where my interests lie, Jon. I suspected something. Russell was always dodgy to me. He's a well-connected man with friends in high and low places."

"You thought he was a part of a group? A fraternity?"

"Something like that."

"A cult?" Jon pressed, well aware of where Nathan's thoughts usually took him.

"I don't know. I suspected ties to a criminal enterprise at least, but my superiors at the time didn't agree. They wanted me to leave Russell well alone, but I wasn't going to sit by and do nothing. So I snuck into Russell's garden and... I saw something. A gathering of some kind, and I thought I saw someone get hurt. Killed maybe. I called it in, but that's when Russell's security found me."

"And how did that pan out?"

"We found nothing in the house. No sign of anyone getting hurt, but back then, I wouldn't hear of it. I became obsessed. Within weeks, I was investigated and demoted, and Alan Peck went to jail for Steed's murder. He claims false imprisonment to this day."

"To this day?"

"I went to see Alan yesterday."

"Why?"

"I was looking back through the files about that case, about what had happened. I was sure that Russell was dodgy, that he was involved in... something. Something more than just a legitimate business. I was also sure that Alan knew a lot more about Russell than he was letting on, but he wouldn't tell us anything back then. I went to see if he wanted to tell us anything new, anything more.

"And did he?"

"No."

"So why did you think he would?"

"Because I was also sure that Alan had been a part of whatever group Russell was a part of, but had been basically kicked out."

"So, what did this group want? Was it like one of these business breakfast groups that meet up for a fried breakfast once a week? Some of those have some pretty silly rules and practices

Nathan smiled incredulously. "Power was their objective, and if I'm right, they'd go so far as killing people to get it."

Jon nodded. "Some people will do anything for a top-drawer fry-up. Their black pudding must have really been something."

"Yeah, I bet it was killer."

"So, did Alan tell you anything?"

"Not much, no. He just suggested that Russell had some questionable friends."

"Questionable friends? Did you get anything else?"

"No, that's all, but I'm convinced he knows more."

Jon nodded. He had a feeling that Russell was involved in something, but he wasn't sure what. "I need a little bit more to go on than a hunch."

"I know, I know," Nathan admitted. "But Alan isn't much of a fan of us, or the police. I did what I could, but he wouldn't say any more than that."

"Isn't there any way to get more out of him?"

"Maybe, but I just don't have that kind of leverage. He thinks we can't do anything against Russell. He thinks we're powerless against someone with that kind of money, so why help us? Plus, he'd be helping the very people who put him in prison. I don't think there's any way he'll help the police, but maybe he doesn't need to. I think we can infer enough from what he did say and keep digging."

"For now."

"I just want some more proof. I need to find the case files about the other missing girls."

"Well, keep going. Look for anything dodgy about Russell. Harassment reports, fraud, dodgy business deals, connections to organised crimes, anything, and let me know if and when you find something, okay?"

"Will do, guv."

20

Leaving him to it, Jon walked towards the exit, glad to see that Nathan had found another angle on the case and was working it to see what he could find.

The Alan side of things was less condemning, but if he could find one or more similar cases of girls going missing related to Russell in some way, that could be the key to bringing this thing home. It could also eliminate Jacob from the case.

That troubled him though. Jacob was clearly an arsehole, who had no respect for women or the law, and the sooner they found and arrested him, the better. Even if he had nothing to do with Olivia's disappearance.

Same with Vassili. He and Jacob were two peas in a pod it seemed, and he'd dearly love to throw them behind bars sooner rather than later.

Stepping out into the main basement corridor, Jon looked up to see Sydney standing a short distance away. She looked a little lost and very out of place in her fitted knee-length black dress and shiny red heels.

"Oh, hello. Fancy seeing you here."

"Excuse me, but what are you doing down here?" Jon asked. Was there no security in this place at all? he thought.

"I was told there was a bathroom I could use, but I think I've got a little lost."

"I should say so, there is a loo in there," Jon said, pointing to the nearby door to the ladies changing rooms beside the gym.

"Oh, of course, how silly of me," she replied with a smile. "I'm not sure I need it now. It's good to see *you* again though, Jon."

"Detective Pilgrim, Miss."

"Of course. Do you like taking charge, Mr Pilgrim?"

Jon narrowed his eyes at her, his internal alarm bells ringing loud and clear. "Are you going to use the facilities or not?"

"How's the hunt for the girl, going?"

"I don't think that's any of your business," Jon replied, finding her word games perplexing and wondering what she was getting at. Her eyes were locked on his, watching him keenly like a predator studies its prey. Kate was right, this was a dangerous woman, and if his suspicions were correct, she was much more dangerous than Russell would ever be, but in a much more insidious way. She looked away from him briefly as she got a little closer. "What do you want?"

Her eyes snapped back to him, and she took a sudden few steps towards him, backing him up against the wall. "You,

Detective Pilgrim. I'd quite like you," she said, placing one hand against the wall, beside his head.

Attempting an answer, Jon found his voice had chosen that moment to piss off on holiday, and leave him mouthing nonsense in reply. Clamping his mouth shut for a moment, Jon blinked a couple of times in shock. What had just happened?

"What's the matter, cat got your tongue, Detective?"

Jon's voice returned with its tail between its legs and he pushed away from the wall, and forced her to take a step back. "I'm flattered, Miss Willow, I am. But I'm afraid I'm spoken for."

"Oh really? And here I was about to offer you the chance of a lifetime. It's not that ginger detective is it? Detective O'Connell? I doubt she could offer you what I can."

"And what's that, herpes?"

Sydney narrowed her eyes. "Careful, Detective. I don't scare easily."

"Neither do I," Jon replied, his voice serious and laced with a note of threat. "And I don't react kindly to being cornered."

"All I have to do is squeal," she replied casually. "I wonder how my millionaire boyfriend and the assistant chief constable would react to some serious allegations."

All humour drained from his face as he stared at her. "Try it, we're on camera."

"I don't think so. I don't think that's required. I have what I came here for, and for that, I thank you."

"What you came here for?"

"A-hem," came a cough from further up the corridor.

Jon turned to see Kate wandering towards them, and felt his cheeks begin to burn.

"Not interrupting anything, am I?"

"Not really," Sydney replied.

"No, nothing," Jon added. "Sydney was just asking me about Russell and the case," he replied, wondering what Kate might think of the mildly compromising situation she'd found him in.

"Was she?" Kate replied, a clear note of suspicion in her voice. "I think you should re-join your partner. He's just upstairs."

"An excellent idea," Sydney replied and stepped away, before looking back at Jon. "It's been magical, Jon."

"Hmmm," Jon muttered in reply. What was it about her that had managed to fluster him so much? He was the detective, the one with the power, he should be leading these conversations and holding her to account, but she seemed to be able to reverse that dynamic in an instant.

He watched her go, swanning up the hallway and then up the stairs, glancing back once with a smile on her face, before she rose out of sight.

"I told you she's trouble," Kate remarked.

"No shit, Sherlock."

"They both are. I can see what they're doing."

"You can?" Jon asked, intrigued.

"Russell was flirting with me the whole time upstairs. Touching my arm and hand, reciting all these little innuendos all the time. He even offered me a ride in his Lamborghini."

Jon laughed. "And you didn't take it?"

She smirked. "I was tempted, sure. It's a Lambo, so…"

"Heh."

"I bet she was doing the same to you, wasn't she? Trying to seduce you. I saw how close she was to you."

"Yeah," Jon nodded. "Too close."

"They're doing it on purpose. They know we're close to something and they're trying to intimidate us. Showing how they can get to us, even here, in the station."

That was not a bad theory, Jon thought. "So, you think they're working together?"

"I think they're trying to protect their interests."

Kate might be onto something, and he was sure Russell would do whatever it took to protect himself and his lifestyle. It was possible that he'd even roped Sydney into it too. But he had a feeling that Sydney was working her own angle on things.

Jon's phone buzzed in his pocket. "Yeah?" he said, answering it, wondering what twist was about to rear its ugly face.

21

"Jeez, this case," Jon remarked as they strode along the hospital corridor, dodging between patients, nurses, and consultants, following the signs and directions they'd been given. "It's starting to really mess with my head. But we need to remain focused on Olivia. It's important we don't lose sight of what we're trying to do."

"I know," Kate replied. "Russell Hodges' involvement has really put a new spin on it. His connections to the police and the power he wields... This one's getting complicated. I never thought I'd see the day when a superior officer would give a suspect a guided tour."

"I'm still trying to process that one myself," Jon replied, and couldn't help but laugh. "The more things that happen, the more I think that Nathan's on to something with his theories."

"Hah, yeah, maybe. So, I forgot to ask, did you find him?"

"He was in the records room. He thinks he remembers an old missing girl case that was linked to Russell."

"Oh, so he might have done this before? Interesting."

"If it's him," Jon countered.

"True. We don't know that yet."

"It would certainly be a damning bit of extra evidence, that's for sure. If Fox can find it."

Kate nodded. "He's like a dog with a bone when he gets a whiff of something. If it's there, he'll find it."

"Hopefully sooner rather than later," Jon remarked, checking the signs. "Is it this way?"

"I think so, yeah, through there," Kate urged, and they walked in into the ward and up to the reception desk. The duty nurse showed them through into a room with six beds and Jon spotted Olivia's mum right away, sitting beside a bed. In it, a man whose face was bandaged was laid up and wearing a hospital gown. Only his eyes and a few bits of skin were visible, but Jon could see the purple bruises and the black eyes he had.

Sylvie stood to greet them. "Oh, you came. Thank you."

"Of course," Jon replied. "Are you okay?"

"Bearing up, I suppose. I'm not the one who was nearly killed, though."

"How is he?" Kate asked.

Sylvie sighed. "He'll survive, but they really hurt him. I just..." Sylvie's voice cracked, and she buried her head in her hands, fighting back tears. Kate went straight in and gave her a hug. Behind her, Geoff looked up, and reached for her. She felt his touch and took hold of his hand.

"It's okay. You're safe here," Kate reassured her, giving Jon a look.

"I just don't know how anyone can do that, it's monstrous," Sylvie said. "And in our own home. I don't know how I can go back there."

"Do you have anywhere you can stay for a few days?"

"I think so, yes," Sylvie replied, sniffing and getting her emotions under control again.

"Can you tell us what happened?" Jon asked. Geoff was looking over at them, and gave a hesitant wave with his hand. Jon nodded back.

"Geoff, lay back. Let me do the talking. You need to rest."

Geoff sighed, relenting. There wasn't much fight in him.

"We woke up to the sound of someone in the house," Sylvie said. "We had no idea who it was, but they came upstairs and went into Olivia's room. We thought it might be..." Her voice caught again from the emotion.

"Olivia," Kate said.

Sylvie nodded. "So Geoff went to have a look, but it wasn't, and they beat him up. They attacked him, and then they ran."

"Do you know who they were?"

"No, sorry, I didn't see them. I stayed in our bedroom and called the police."

"Okay. What about Geoff, can he talk?"

"He can, but it hurts him after a while."

Looking over, Geoff tried to lift his head. "I… I can talk…ugh." He hissed in pain.

Raising his hands, Jon waved him back down. "No, stop. You lie there. Just raise your hand for yes, do nothing for no. Okay?"

Geoff raised his hand.

"Okay, good. Did you see their faces?"

No movement.

"Okay, so do you know who they were?" Jon asked.

Again, no movement.

"Was there more than one?"

Geoff's hand rose.

"Okay, good. How many?"

"At least two," Sylvie cut in. I think maybe I heard three, but I can't be sure."

"You saw two?" Jon asked. Geoff raised his hand. "Okay. I think we have a forensic team going over your place," he said, looking over at Kate.

"That's right, Sheridan's there now."

"Excellent. Which means if there's any evidence, we'll find it."

"Did they take anything?" Kate asked.

"No, they took nothing. I checked," Sylvie answered.

"Okay, so they came in, and went to Olivia's room, and ran once they'd been disturbed, but not before taking the time to beat up your husband. Is that about right?"

"I think so," Sylvie replied.

"And they never came to find you? They didn't go into your room?"

"I was hiding in the corner, so they might have looked in our room, but they didn't try to find me," Sylvie answered.

"Interesting," Jon replied, and looked over at Kate, who sported a similar frown to Jon's as she processed this information. They asked a few more questions, but were soon on their way out, leaving Geoff to get some much-earned rest.

"My guess," Jon said as they walked back out through the hospital, "is that they were either looking for Olivia, or they wanted something from her room, but were disturbed."

"What would they want from her room?" Kate asked.

"I've got no idea," Jon remarked.

"No, I think it was the first option."

"Okay, so who was it?"

"Jacob? Vassili, maybe?"

"If you're right, that means they didn't kidnap her," Jon replied. "Which means someone else did."

"Russell?"

Jon shrugged. "Maybe."

"Hmm. I think we're missing a piece of the puzzle here."

"You and me both," he replied and pulled out his phone which had started to ring. It was the station again. "It never rains, but it pours," he said, answering. "Yes?"

22

Walking back into the SIU office, Jon spotted Rachel walking over.

"Aaah, you're back," she said.

"Well spotted, Detective, you'll go far," Jon answered. "So what's all this about Lily and her parents?"

"They've come in, they want to speak to you. Sounds like they've had a visitor."

"A visitor? To their house? Huh, curious. Like Geoff and Sylvie did."

"Could just be a coincidence," Kate suggested.

"I don't believe in coincidences where my cases are concerned."

"You sound like Nathan."

"What? Oh, crap, no. Well, I might allow one or two coincidences, you know? Nothing major, though."

"Nice save."

"I know, right? Nothing gets past me. You've got to get up pretty early to pull the wool over my eyes."

"They're downstairs, in the same room they were in last time," Rachel said.

"I'm boasting here, DS Arthur. Never interrupt me when I'm boasting."

"Noted, sir," Rachel replied with a roll of her eyes, much to Jon's amusement.

"Good, never let it happen again."

"When you've quite finished, shall we go and see what's up with Lily?" Kate asked, her hands on her hips as she raised an eyebrow at him.

"Jeez, you're no fun. Right then, let's go and see what's up."

"I'm fun," Kate protested as they set off down to the meeting room. "Just, appropriately fun."

"Clearly that's the best kind of fun."

"I think so. You're in rare form at the moment."

Jon sighed. "Just finding moments of levity where I can. I'll go crazy if I don't."

"I hear yeh," Kate agreed, as they headed downstairs and walked into the room where Lily and her parents waited for them.

"Hi, how are you doing?" Kate asked, Lily.

She sat on the sofa, wringing her hands, while her leg bounced with nervous energy. She looked up and smiled briefly. "Yeah, okay I guess."

"Are we alright to ask some questions?" Jon asked.

"I...err, I *wanted* to talk to you, actually," Lily replied.

"We had a visitor," Myles added.

"Myles, let her tell it," Nina scolded him.

"Okay, okay. Sorry."

Nina shook her head in despair. "Sorry, Detective."

"That's okay. In your own time, Lily."

She nodded, her leg still bouncing as she looked to her floor for a moment. "Yana came to the house."

"When did this happen?" He needed to know the timeline.

"This morning. She just knocked on the door. Mum answered it, and she said she was a school friend who'd heard I was home. So I came to the door. I don't know why I did that really. I should have known something was up right then. I don't really have any school friends. Not anymore, anyway." Lily paused and seemed to clam up for a moment.

"It's okay, take your time," Kate reassured her. "So what did she say to you?"

Lily sniffed and blinked some tears away. "She warned me. She told me to keep my mouth shut about Vassili, and the house. She said if I said anything, they'd find me and hurt me and my parents."

"She threatened you?"

"She'd do it, too. I know she would," Lily replied. "I know what they're like. I've seen it. I'm scared."

"Look, we'll do what we can to help. We can post an officer at your house or put you up somewhere for a bit."

"Can you?" Nina asked. "That would be amazing."

"I didn't really want to admit this, but I am a little worried about being in the house," Myles added. "Is that silly?"

"No," Jon said. "There's nothing to be embarrassed about when it comes to things like this. These are hardened criminals, who will do whatever they need to, to hold onto their power, so you have every right to be worried."

"Okay, thank you. I really appreciate it."

"That's okay. We'll sort something out for you."

"So, how did this visit by Yana end?" Kate asked Lily.

"When she threatened me, I told her to… pee off, you know? I slammed the door in her face."

"I understand," Kate replied. "That was really brave of you."

Lily gave a nervous laugh. "Heh, thanks. I just… I know what they're capable of and it worries me."

"You're okay now. And thank you for telling us."

"But that's not all. I want to tell you everything," Lily said. "I don't care what Yana wants. I want to stop them, and I think I can help you. Is that okay?"

"You can tell us whatever you like," Kate answered.

"Okay, well… I'm sorry I didn't say this when I was last here, but I was scared. I thought it was best, so I kept quiet. But then last night, I just couldn't sleep. My mind was racing, thinking about the others. I came to the conclusion that I either needed to help, and tell you what I knew, or live with that guilt for the rest of my life. But I can't do that. I'm a mess as it is without more guilt added in. After Yana visited, that was the final straw. I needed to end this."

"And we're glad you chose to come and talk to us," Kate replied. "We'll protect you as best we can, okay?"

"Yeah."

"Take your time, we're listening."

"We were brainwashed. I know that sounds silly, and it took me a long time to realise it. I think Olivia came to the same conclusion before I did, I just didn't want to admit it to myself. I couldn't, because that would mean I had been wrong, that I'd made a mistake. That's not something that's easy to admit. But Olivia helped me with that, so I have her to thank. When she left, something changed for me over the next day. I suddenly knew the truth. Coming here and seeing my mum and dad again. It all seemed so obvious.

"They lured us in. It took a while, and it happened over the months when we kept running away from home. Jacob and his friends, Tyler and Zack, they had money and looked after us. They kept buying us stuff—clothes and jewellery, all sorts. Whatever we wanted, it was ours. They just had so much money. And I know, it's stupid and so shallow, but that mixed with what I thought was a genuine friendliness and understanding, was appealing.

"They lured us away from our friends. They kept telling us how they were jealous, how my mum and dad didn't care about me as much as they did. And I believed it. When I was with them, they seemed to understand us. I just felt a connection. They were there for us, helped us. Treated us like adults. I didn't want to go to school, I hated it. So Jacob made the most of that too, and we stopped going. It felt rebellious, freeing. I loved it. It was kind of intoxicating. I got quite close to Olivia. She'd been with Jacob for a while then, and I think she believed it all. She was as bad as the boys were in trying to get me to move out and in with her. But I don't blame her. She was just caught in that web already. A true believer.

"And then she got me to take some drugs. It was stupid but it was just a bit of fun, you know? She'd had them before and told me how great they were and how she'd look after me. So I thought, why not? What harm can it do? That first trip, it was good, actually. I quite enjoyed it. When I moved in with her, into Jacob's place, we started using more often. Looking back now, I think she did it to hide from her pain. I think they were already abusing her."

"In what way?" Kate asked.

"Like, you know. Getting her drugged up, and then doing what they wanted with her while she was knocked out or delirious."

"You mean, raping her?"

Lily flushed and looked uncomfortable. "I think so. She never really told me. I just… I saw the pain in her eyes. She was broken inside. They did that to her. I wish I'd seen it earlier. I wish I'd known. I should've been stronger."

"You did nothing wrong, Lily," Kate said. "They did this. Remember that. They took advantage of you and Olivia. They are the predators. They're the ones in the wrong."

"Did they do the same to you?" Jon asked, feeling so terribly sorry for her, while also feeling a boiling, white-hot rage and hatred for the lowlifes that were responsible. They didn't deserve to live on this Earth, frankly. He'd seen so many people whose lives were left in utter ruin by stuff like this, and it always made him so angry. But, he had a job to do. He couldn't give in to his wrath. Instead, he needed to channel it and use it. It was fuel for him to hunt people like this down, and stop them.

"I think they were planning to. I… I have blacked out a few times from the drugs, so… I don't know."

Jon wanted to help Lily in whatever way he could, and he could see the pain and confusion behind her eyes. Her mother hugged Lily close, doing the very thing that Jon wanted to, but wouldn't. It wasn't his or Kate's place to comfort anyone like that, no matter how much they wanted to help and save them from the horrors they'd experienced. He'd had training in how to handle victims, but he wasn't a specialist in these things. There were others better suited to that task, and he and his team would make sure that Lily, and hopefully Olivia, got the best care possible. In the meantime, it was down to him and his team to do what they did best, and find those responsible, and bring them to justice.

"Can you tell us about anything else that goes on in that house?" Jon asked.

"They're involved in all sorts," Lily said, sniffing as Nina pulled away from her. "There's usually always drugs of some kind there. I think that's Vassili's main thing. He's a dealer, but I think there's more. I think there might be other people...other girls there."

"Girls like you? That they've groomed and gaslighted?" Jon asked.

"I've not met them, but I've heard Russian being spoken, and screams..."

"Anything else?"

"They have weapons. I've seen guns a few times. Lots of people come and go too. I don't know who they are, but they're not very nice most of the time. They say disgusting things. I tried to keep away from it, though. They scared me. Everything scared me after a while. It all started off nice. None of that stuff was on display when we first got there. But it just got worse and worse as the months passed."

"Is that why you ran? Because you were scared?"

179

Lily nodded. "When Olivia left, there was nothing there for me anymore, and I saw the lie of it. Olivia had been the one telling me to go there, to move in, to leave my parents. When she left, when she said how much she hated it all, I knew I had to go too."

"But you stayed another night," Kate replied with a frown.

"I know. But I was terrified. I was scared of what would happen when I left. Also, I thought Olivia would come back. I didn't think she'd actually leave and not come back."

"But she did," Jon replied.

"She did. So I had to leave, too. I had to find her."

"And that led you here," Jon remarked.

Lily nodded.

"Thank you, Lily," Jon said. "You've been a great help. I really appreciate what you've given us, and you have my promise that we will find Olivia and bring Jacob and the others to justice."

"Thank you."

"I'll arrange for someone to help you with an official statement if that's okay?"

Lily nodded again. "I want to help."

"Good. Thank you."

Walking back towards the office, with Kate by his side, his mind running through the events that Lily had recounted, he knew they needed to act fast. "I need that warrant," he muttered. "I need to get into that house."

23

"Rachel?" Jon called out as he strode towards his office.

"Guv?"

"Where's my warrant?"

"I'll chase it up now," she replied, made to make a phone call, and then turned back to him. "Oh, and Nathan's in the incident room. I think he has something for you."

Jon stopped in his tracks and glanced over at Kate, who shared a look of surprise and hope. "Thank you, Rachel. Coming, Kate?"

"Damn right," she replied and followed him across the office towards the incident room where, sure enough, Nathan waited for them, sitting at the table.

Was it too much to hope that Nathan had found something so damning that they could finally pin this on someone? Probably, but that didn't stop him from hoping for something mind-blowing.

"You've found something?" Jon asked as he walked into the room, followed by Kate.

Standing, Nathan nodded. "*Something*, yes. I've found *something*."

"Well, that's better than nothing. Okay, spill it. What have you got?"

"Firstly, it's not what I thought it was. I had another case in mind, but this one cropped up during my search, and it seems to fit."

"Go on," Jon replied, tantalised by the idea that there might be more where this came from.

"Okay, so several years ago, a young woman called Iryna comes over here from Poland looking for work. She did well for herself and worked a couple of jobs before being employed by RH Enterprises, Russell's company. She worked there for several months and according to everyone who knew her, excelling at her job until one day, she just didn't turn up. They looked into it, but she'd disappeared. Not only that, but she was never found.

"During the police investigation, several employees said they believed they witnessed several instances of sexual harassment against Iryna, committed by Russell. However, they were looked into, and nothing stuck. Most ended up withdrawing their statements, and everything ended up just fizzling away. Plus, he had some corroborating alibis for everything that came up, putting him elsewhere for a bunch of them, and giving alternate witnesses to others, including for the period that Iryna went missing. She's still missing today."

"I can believe every word of those employees," Kate said. "He's a real slime ball, and was a little too handsy with me during that ridiculous tour."

"If the glove fits," Jon agreed and looked over at Kate. "I saw how he was with you, so I can believe the harassment reports. I can also see him using his considerable wealth and power to make those allegations disappear."

"He can just throw money at the problem," Kate agreed. "Most people don't want to lose their jobs and be sued to kingdom come."

"If we end up taking him down, I bagsy the Shelby Cobra I saw in his garage."

"Ooh, I'll take his Lambo," Kate joined in with a smile.

"So, you don't think that's the only case that supports ours against him?" Jon said.

"It's not the one I remember, no. I'm sure I remember one that was similar to ours with someone going missing a day or so after she'd spent an evening with him and his entourage out on the town. I'll keep looking, though."

"Thank you, Fox."

"Any updates on the case?" Nathan asked.

"Lily's just come back and told us about the house of horrors she's been living in for the best part of a year. Plus, Olivia's parents had their house broken into and her father was assaulted. We think someone was there looking for Olivia."

"Sounds like you have your hands full. Right, I'll get back to it. Keep your fingers crossed," Nathan replied and walked out the room.

"What do you think?" Jon asked.

"It's another little bit of weight on our side of the scales," Kate replied.

"Right. It's hardly damning, but if we can build up our weight of evidence, it'll only stand us in good stead once the case makes it to court."

"Every little bit helps," Kate said. Stepping up to him, she asked, "How're you holding up?"

"I'm okay," he replied. "Looking forward to Friday night."

"Oh?" Kate replied. "And what's happening on Friday night?"

Surprised, Jon gave her a look waiting to see if she'd say anything, but she only looked at him, confused. "But, I thought...?" Jon continued, hoping that Kate hadn't forgotten about their date.

As he watched, a smile spread over her lips. "I'm kidding," she relented finally. "I'm looking forward to it too. So, where will you be taking me?"

Jon felt his stomach fall as he realised he'd not booked a table anywhere. "Oh, me? I thought."

Kate raised her eyebrows at him.

"No, don't worry, I'll sort it. I'll find somewhere."

Kate narrowed her eyes at him. "I'm not eating gravy and chips while sitting on a car again. That's not a date."

"It's *chips and gravy*, not gravy and chips, only a crazy person would say it that way around."

"Whatever, I'm not eating that, sitting out in the cold."

"Yep, no, I know. Leave it with me, all will be fine," Jon replied, feeling utterly panicked by the thought of him calling around and not being able to find a table anywhere. He needed to get on to that as soon as possible. If only this case would let up on him a little bit and give him some breathing room.

"First impressions count for a lot, you know," Kate said.

"Right, yes. They do," Jon agreed. "But we've known each other for a while now, aren't we a little beyond first impressions?"

"We're starting again, remember, Loxley? I'm looking forward to being impressed."

"Oh, jeez," he muttered, being a little melodramatic.

Kate laughed.

Rachel suddenly popped her head in the door of the incident room.

"Sir?"

"DS Arthur, please tell me you have some good news."

She smiled. "I have some good news."

24

"You're going into the home of a career criminal, someone who has links to the Russian Mob, deals drugs, and traffics women. We have credible reports that there might be weapons in there too. So be careful. The main man we're after is called Vassili Syomin, but we're also looking for Yana Perova, Jacob Cole, Tyler Lee, and Zack Porter. You need to arrest and secure anyone you find, but also be aware that there could be victims in there, so be careful, we need to treat them with respect. Understood?"

"Yes, sir," the assembled officers intoned.

His pep talk finished, the armed response unit moved to their van, while everyone else went about their business, either getting in cars or making sure they had everything they needed.

"Rachel," Jon said, spotting a moment without anyone around, while Kate was getting their car ready.

"Sir?"

"Is there a good, local place to go for a nice meal out, such as, on a date, maybe?"

"You're asking me where to take a woman on a date?"

"I don't know the area," Jon protested. "And in case you hadn't noticed, this job is fairly full-on."

"Are you asking me out, sir?"

"No, no, never."

"Never?"

"Um, well, what I mean is. You're a good looking woman and all, but…"

"I'm fucking with you, Jon. Besides, I'm in a relationship."

Jon went to speak, and then sighed. "Thanks for that."

"Anytime, it's the least I can do. Alright, well, I guess there are a few places. Depends on your budget."

"I want to make a good first impression."

"Like I said, there are several places. This is Surrey, remember?"

"Right, yeah. Silly me. Anyway, I can't stay here and chat, but can you find one and book a table for two, under my name?"

Rachel smiled. "Will do, Romeo."

"Thanks," he smiled.

"You've only been here a few weeks," Rachel replied, and then glanced over at Kate, before looking back at him, her eyebrows raised dramatically. "You work quick."

Blushing, Jon shrugged. "When it's right, it's right."

"Heh, yeah. I guess."

"Thank you, Rachel, I owe you one," he said, making for the car.

"Damn right you do," she replied, walking off.

"What was that all about?" Kate asked as he got in the car.

"Just some admin crap," he replied, brushing the comment away. "Right, let's go and get this creep."

Kate nodded and joined the small convoy of vehicles as they headed out.

Making their way through the Surrey countryside, Jon wondered if this action might bring the case to an end. It was by no means certain that Russell had anything to do with Olivia's disappearance, and his link to her was fleeting and superficial at best. But still, there was something about it that felt strangely compelling to him. He was at a loss as to what it might be, though.

Would Jacob be here, hiding in a room somewhere, maybe with Olivia?

Honestly, he hoped so, he needed to find her and bring her home as soon as possible. But he worried that this was just a distraction, and Olivia was nowhere near here, held by someone totally unrelated to any of this.

He hoped she was okay, and that she could hold on for just a little while longer.

He needed to get his head in the game though and focus on what they were going to do next, otherwise, people could die. Storming into the base of a criminal enterprise was never a trivial thing.

Radio chatter back and forth filled the car as the group closed in on the house, approaching from several different directions after splitting up partway. Kate stayed with the main van, following them to the house.

They parked up several roads away and waited for the other parts of the team to get into place. Communication then shifted to the two plain-clothed officers watching the house, who informed them that as far as they knew, Vassili was still in the building.

"That's good news," Kate commented.

"It sure is. Okay, I think it's go-time, unless you can think of a reason not to?"

"Nope, none at all."

Jon nodded and pressed the send button on the pool car's radio. "Let's go."

The order given, the van ahead set off with a brief wheelspin. Jon smiled at the enthusiasm of the armed response team, as Kate followed it around the next few roads before they turned into the driveway.

"They love this part," Jon remarked, as he watched the officers jump out of the van and run towards the house.

"I can tell," Kate replied as they got out and followed.

Wearing his armoured vest and holding his baton, Jon followed the main team up to the house. Within the group, he spotted the officer carrying the large red battering ram they used to break down doors, ready for use.

They continued up the driveway and made for the main door. Jon looked back at Kate, where she stood, right on his heels, her baton in hand.

"Are you ready?"

"Of course, this is hardly my first of these," Kate replied. "Are you?"

"Yep," he answered, but couldn't help feeling a little protective of Kate. He didn't want her getting hurt. He didn't want anyone to get hurt, of course, especially not anyone on his team, but his budding feelings for Kate pulled on his heartstrings that little bit harder.

He needed to get past that, though, if he wanted to keep working with her. If his feelings started to get in the way, then one or both of them would get transferred and he didn't want that. Pushing his feelings of concern away, Jon did his best to focus on the job at hand.

Find Vassili and anyone else who might be here.

"Make way for the big red key," the officer with the ram said as he ran forward. With a big swing, he slammed the ram into the door with an almighty bang. It took four solid hits to get the door open, before the team charged in, shouting about their arrival to the residents.

"Armed police!"

"Hands up!"

"Come out!"

The next few moments were frantic as Jon rushed through the house. A man was quickly thrown to the floor in the entrance hall and cuffed, and in the next room, two more were ordered at gunpoint to get on the ground.

The armed officers were taking no chances. With the report of guns and other weapons in the house, there was no room for error.

Moving through to a back room, a man came charging out of another door holding a large sword aloft. He screamed as he ran, topless and barefoot with only an old pair of jeans on.

"Jesus," Jon gasped.

"Halt!" an officer shouted as they backed off, but the man kept coming. His eyes were wild and bugging out of his skull as he ran.

"Stop or we'll shoot!"

But the man didn't listen and ran towards one of the officers.

An ear-splitting bang rang through the house as one of the team fired. His shoulder hit, blood flew, and the man spun, before staggering. He dropped his sword, which clattered to the floor, before he fell on his arse, his face the picture of shock.

The man turned his head and looked down at his shoulder, which was leaking blood.

"Trippy, man," he muttered and then collapsed in a heap.

Stepping forward, Jon put his foot on the sword, and then kicked it away into a corner. "Bloody hell, what does he think this is? The Middle Ages?"

"Watch him, and secure that bloody sword," one of the lead officers ordered his team and pressed on. In the kitchen at the back of the house, Jon found Vassili sitting at the table, his hands already up, a roll-up hanging from his mouth. He looked unconcerned by the armed officers that were aiming their guns at him.

Vassili noticed them suddenly, and his eyebrows rose up. "Aaah, I wonder when you'd be back."

"I know, I missed you too. I came as quick as I could."

"Ha! How generous of you, comrade."

Done with his remarks, Jon walked up to him, and stared down at him, while armed officers continued to point their MP5s at him.

"Where is he?"

"Where is who, Mr Detective man? Who you talk about?"

"Jacob and his friends, Tyler and Zack."

"How I know that? I not know Jacob. I not know who you talk about."

"Oh, you don't? Well, whatever, I think we'll have enough here to put you away." Jon eyed the bags of white power on the table, along with other drugs paraphernalia.

"You can try, you can try."

"You doubt me?"

"Always. You do not scare me."

"Hmm. Okay, what about Lily? You know Lily, right?"

"Again, you talk silly, Mr Detective. I not know Lily. Who is Lily? There no Lily here."

"Oh, really?" Jon replied.

"You crazy," Vassili replied.

Jon pulled his phone out, hunted for the contact, and then smiled. He showed the screen to Vassili. "What's that say?"

Vassili glanced at the screen, and then at him. He shrugged.

"Lily, it says Lily, and that's her number. Shall we call it? Hmm? She apparently left her phone here, you know? She dropped it when she ran. Let's see, shall we?" He tapped call.

Seconds later, a phone could be heard vibrating nearby. A few seconds worth of searching by the officers who were with him, revealed the phone dumped in a kitchen drawer, along with several others.

Jon ended the call with a smile on his face. "I do find it odd that you say Lily was never here, and yet you somehow have her phone."

Vassili grimaced but said nothing.

"Detectives?" a voice called out.

"Sorry, duty calls," Jon remarked and stepped away from Vassili. "Cuff him."

Jon moved through another door into an adjacent hallway, and as he reached the bottom of the stairway, the voice called out again from above. "Sir? This way, sir." The armed offer at the top of the stairs waved them up. Jon gave Kate a brief look, and then made his way up, following the waiting officer.

"What's up?"

"We've found something I think you should see."

"Okay," he replied. The officer was walking quickly, and Jon nearly had to jog to keep up as they passed several empty rooms on either side. There was another man on the floor, cuffed and being watched. He'd need to find out if any of these men were Jacob. He realised he'd not seen Yana yet, either, but there was much of the sprawling house he'd not seen yet, so she could be anywhere.

Further up, the officer stopped by an open door and ushered them in. Walking inside, Jon came up short as he took in the scene before him while a rank smell assaulted his senses. A female officer was sitting on the edge of the bed, holding the hand of a painfully thin young woman. She looked both malnourished and delirious. Her other hand was above her head, her wrist cuffed to the bed frame. Her clothes were little more than dirty rags and had likely been worn for days or weeks. He could see red-raw injection marks on her arm as her eyes rolled around in her head, not really focusing on anything.

"Jesus," he hissed, shocked and disgusted.

"Oh my God," Kate said, beside him.

"We found her like this," the woman holding the captive's hand said. "She's clearly high. We've got an ambulance on the way. Donovan, where are those bolt cutters?"

"Let me look. Oh, here they come," the officer who'd led them up said and grabbed them from another officer who'd brought them in from the van. Donovan cut the chain on the cuffs, freeing the girl.

"Have you ever seen anything like this before?" Kate asked in hushed tones.

"Unfortunately, yes." He sighed. "He must have known we'd find her up here."

"Vassili? Yeah. Maybe he doesn't care, though."

"Donovan, is it? Was this the only captive you found?"

"Yes, sir. Although, we did find several empty bedrooms just like this one. I think he had more in here not too long ago."

"Shit. Well, saving one's better than none."

"Why didn't he move her?" Kate asked.

"Maybe we were watching him by then? I don't know. Okay, let's have a look around and make sure we've not missed anything."

25

Walking into his office, Jon slapped the file down on his desk, placed his fists on his hips, and sighed. He closed his eyes in frustration and took a moment to calm himself.

"No luck?"

Jon turned to see Kate, a sympathetic and friendly, if slightly sheepish smile on her face.

"Nope. Not really," he replied. "Tyler said basically nothing."

"Zack was the same," she replied. To speed things up, she'd interviewed Zack at the same time, and it sounded like she'd not got much further with him. Kate perched on the edge of his desk beside him. "He didn't say a word to me, apart from his name and 'no comment.' We'll get them, though."

"I hope so," he said smiling at her. He'd spent the last hour or so in a small interview room with Jacob's accomplice, and frankly, he might as well have been talking to a brick wall. He'd probably have got more out of the wall, too. Tyler had refused to answer most of the questions put to him, saying only, 'no comment'.

His lawyer, who'd delayed the interview by being late, and then by taking his time in deliberations, had sat beside him.

The Solicitor had a smug grin on his face half the time that Jon wanted to punch clean off his face and into next week.

Tyler had confirmed his name, age, and other personal details, and about one of the only questions he had answered was that he didn't know where Jacob was. He'd not seen him in days and wasn't actually that friendly with him, apparently.

It all sounded far too much like these were scripted answers given to him by his representation. The solicitor wasn't one of the random duty ones, like Ana, either. No, Tyler knew the name and details of the person he wanted representing him, which was all the more suspicious when it became clear that his, Zack's, and Vassili's solicitors were all from the same company.

Jon had eventually just given up for the time being and would delegate the interview to someone else for the moment.

"Any news?" Jon asked.

"Nothing yet," Kate admitted. "We don't know where Jacob or Olivia are, Nathan's not come back with anything incriminating, Vassili's still talking to his lawyer, and there's no news on Russell, either."

That worried him. "We have embarrassingly few leads on this one," Jon stated. "Or, that's what it feels like."

"We've got a few," Kate replied.

"Nothing concrete, yet."

"No. But who knows? Maybe Vassili will have something to say."

"I doubt it, but we can hope, I suppose," Jon replied as he turned and looked out into the office.

"Maybe you just need to go home and have a good night's sleep," Kate suggested. "Come at it fresh in the morning."

"A full and restful night's sleep would be lovely about now, that's for sure. I rarely sleep all the way through these days. My mind's always racing with thoughts about the day's events, and trying to figure out the best way forward on the case."

"I'm the same. I think most of us are, to be honest."

"Yeah, I know. I'm very grateful to you all. I think I've really landed on my feet with this team."

"Wait! Hold on a cotton-picking minute there. Is that a compliment, Pilgrim?"

"Well, maybe just a small one."

"Who are you, and what have you done with Jon!?"

"I'm just being nice, Barry."

"My comment still stands. I don't think I know who you are."

"Shut it, Finger-Girl."

"That's Finger-Woman, to you!"

"Finger who?" said a voice from the door.

Jon turned to see Debby Constable, one of the civilian office workers employed at the station at the door, looking a little bewildered. "We're just discussing superhero names. You know, serious police work."

"Riiight."

"She's Finger-Girl—"

"Finger-Woman, Jon, Finger-Woman."

"Whatever. And I'm…" Jon pondered the idea, tapping his chin with his finger.

"Gravy-Boy," Kate cut in, grinning.

"Gravy-Man, actually."

"Glad to see you're taking things seriously," Debby said.

"This is grave and important work, Constable. I wouldn't have slept tonight if this hadn't been resolved."

"Well, I have a little more work for you caped crusaders. Vassili has finished talking to his solicitor, and is ready to see you."

"Oh, how wonderful, I'm sure this will be just as fulfilling and rewarding an experience as it was talking to Tyler."

"And Zack," Kate added.

"Want to tackle it together?" Jon suggested to Kate.

"Sure, why not? He'll never be able to resist the tag team of Gravy-Man and Finger-Woman!"

"I think you need a new name, Kate," Debby said. "That one raises far too many questions."

"Nonsense, I won't hear of it," Jon remarked. "Come, Finger-Woman, adventure awaits. Ne'er-do-wells and criminal masterminds will quake in their boots at the sound of our names. They'll whisper about us in the shadows, fearing that we'll come for them this night."

"I think you've taken this analogy about as far as it can go," Debby commented.

"Do not underestimate my power, woman! I can drag this out for weeks yet."

"Oh, I believe it. I'll leave you to it. I have actual work to be getting on with," Debby replied and walked away.

"I don't think she appreciated our humour," Kate remarked.

"Those weak-of-mind, rarely do, ol' buddy, ol' chum."

Kate merely stared at him, blinking a couple of times. "You're suggesting I'm *your* sidekick, right? And yet you know I'm clearly superior."

"Don't make me pull rank, Barry. Come on, let's get this over with," he replied and set off for the interview rooms with Kate beside him.

Sure enough, they found Vassili in interview room three, sitting alongside an older man in a prim business suit with little hint of a personality. Jon ran through the basics, introducing himself and Kate, and reading Vassili his rights, before getting him to confirm his name.

"Vassili Syomin," he replied in his thick Russian accent.

"Good. We've brought you here on suspicion of kidnapping, human trafficking, possession with intent to supply drugs, as well as having several illegal weapons within your house. How do you explain yourself?"

"No comment."

Jon's heart sank, feeling sure he knew how this was going to go, but there really was nothing for it. They had to proceed, but for now, he decided to take a different route and focus on the main issue they wanted resolving.

"When did Olivia Cook leave the house?"

"Who's that?"

Jon resisted a grimace, as Vassili dodged the trap. "Olivia Cook. She's been living in your house for the best part of a year. She was brought in by Jacob."

"I not know this girl."

"You're saying you have no knowledge of Olivia Cook?"

"No."

"What about Lily Austin?"

Vassili shook his head.

"You had her phone in your kitchen," Jon stated.

"I not know where that come from. Nothing to do with me."

Jon narrowed his eyes. "Both these young women state categorically that they've been living in your house for the best part of a year, and you're saying you have no knowledge of them?"

"I rent out rooms to people who can afford them. What they do in rooms is up to them. I not interfere as long as they pay. I not ask questions, I not go snooping around their rooms, I leave them to it. If they bring girl back to room, it not my business."

"Given it's your house, I'd say it's very much your business," Jon remarked.

"I disagree."

"So, you're saying that Jacob was your tenant?"

"I not know him well. He was tenant for a while, but that all, and I not see him in days. Besides, he late with rent, so I throw him out, anyway."

"You've not seen Jacob in days?"

"No."

"How well do you know Tyler Lee and Zack Porter?"

"Tenants, like Jacob. I not know well."

"Are you sure about that?"

"Very sure."

"What about Yana?" Kate asked.

"Who Yana?"

"The young woman who answered your door when we visited you the first time? That Yana?" Kate clarified

"Just another tenant."

"And where is she?"

Vassili smiled. "I not know." He looked very pleased by the fact that they had not arrested Yana.

"You seemed very friendly with her when we stopped by the other day," Jon joined in.

"I friendly with everyone, when they nice to me."

"Are we not being nice to you, Vassili?"

You try to make me think I do bad things, but I only do good things. I help, I rent rooms at cheap price. I not bad."

"I think I beg to differ, there, Vassili," Jon replied.

"Tell us about the girl we found upstairs," Kate asked. "She was chained to the bed, malnourished, bruised, and hurt. You're saying you didn't have any idea about her?"

Vassili shrugged, and Jon rolled his eyes. He knew where this interview was going, and it felt incredibly draining knowing how much trouble they'd clearly have with him. Right now, he was walking pretty much in lockstep with Tyler and Zack, trying to frustrate the process.

But they did have Lily's statement, and once she was well enough, they'd have the statement from the girl they'd found too. But none of these would bring them any closer to finding Olivia, Jon's ultimate goal.

Jon shifted in his seat, settling in for what seemed would be a long and annoying interview.

26

It was late by the time Jon got back to the hotel, his current home until he could finally buy one of his own. He'd considered getting a flat to rent, but the force was still happy to contribute to the hotel. So, until that changed, and it likely would very soon, he was happy where he was. Walking in, he checked his messages and saw he'd missed some calls from the estate agents, and vowed to call them back tomorrow.

The owners of the house he liked were negotiating hard, which had led to an offer and counter-offer situation that was draining to think about.

Stuffing his phone back in his pocket, Jon wondered where this case would end up going. Vassili was steadfastly denying any knowledge of the stuff that was going on in his house, which was to Jon's mind, patently ridiculous, but who knew how these things would play out in court. It would be the word of two young ladies who'd been victimised, versus the powerful, well-funded lawyers who were backed by a criminal organisation.

Things did not look great. But if they could add Olivia in too, then that was three against them. The more they could bring in, the better.

Still, the process of going over all the details and having Vassili just throw it back in his face had left him drained, and he was looking forward to a good night's rest.

As he walked up to his door, his phone buzzed, alerting him to a message. Unlocking the door, he checked the screen as he walked in, reading a short text from Rachel.

'I've booked the Ivy Cobham Brasserie at 8 pm on Friday. Let me know if that's okay."

The Ivy? It certainly sounded nice.

"Important message?"

Jon looked up to see Sydney sat at the small table in his hotel room. She held a glass of wine in her hand, the half-drunk bottle beside her, its fruity aroma filling the room.

"What the hell?" Jon remarked, looking around his room and then back to her. "What are you doing? How did you get in here?"

"Shush, Jon. You'll wake the neighbours. Come, have a drink with me."

"Like hell, I will. Get out!"

"Now, that's just rude, Jon. But, I'll let it slide. I understand that this might have come as something of a shock, and that's fine. But I found that I just had to come and see you."

"What are you talking about?"

"I like you, Jon."

"You don't know me."

"Oh, I'm not so sure. You became a detective at a young age and rose through the ranks, becoming one of the youngest officers to ever become a DCI. That's impressive, Jon. Very impressive."

"You've been investigating me?"

She shrugged. "What can I say? I like to know about the men I take an interest in. And you've led an interesting life. For instance, I must express my condolences for your girlfriend, Charlotte. That must have been difficult."

Jon narrowed his eyes at her, but didn't reply.

"A sensitive subject, I understand. Let's move on to your hunt for serial killers, shall we? Because that is really, very interesting."

"Is it?"

"Oh yes. I mean, that's why you're down here, right? That's why you joined the SIU?"

"That's right," he replied, wondering where she was going with this.

"Well, I might be able to help you."

"With what?"

"With Olivia, of course. I might be able to help you find her."

"Is that right?" Was she lying?

"Don't be so suspicious, Jon. I bear you no ill will."

Her word games were tiring, and he was starting to lose his patience with her. "Get to the point, Sydney."

She seemed to sense that and stood. Walking over, she came close, taking a sip from her wine glass. "I have a lead to follow up, on a personal matter, but providing that pans out, I think I might be able to help you get what you need."

"You're saying Russell's involved?"

"I never said that," she replied, and then smiled. "Russell's an interesting man, but my ambitions are much bigger than just him." She raised a hand and traced her finger along his tie. "You intrigue me, Jon Pilgrim. A keen, dogged detective, not afraid to stand up to the rich and powerful. I like that."

"Like I said before, I'm currently in a relati—"

She pulled the tie, yanking his head closer, and kissed him.

Jon pulled away instantly and backed up, shocked. "Get off me."

"That was nice," she replied.

"Get out."

"I'm going to be a very rich woman, Jon. Very rich. You could share that with me. I don't want to be alone, you know."

"I have no interest in you beyond this case," Jon replied. "Now please leave."

"Think about it, Jon. I will be in touch shortly. Enjoy the wine," she replied, placing her empty glass down on the side table, and walking past him to the exit.

She glanced back once as she walked out, a wicked smile on her ruby lips. And then she was gone.

"Holy fuck," Jon cursed, releasing a long breath as he sank down onto the bed. What the hell was that all about? How on earth could she be interested in him, they'd only met twice before?

She was stunning, that was true, just as Kate had said, but beauty was only skin deep, and she seemed as crazy as they came.

But the woman was quite clearly a conniving, dangerous person, and he really didn't want anything to do with her. However, he was also quite sure this wouldn't be the last he would see of her.

Turning, he regarded the bottle on the table. For a moment, he briefly considered having a drink, but then decided not to and poured it down the bathroom sink.

His bed was calling him, and he had no desire to resist it.

27

Opening her eyes, Olivia woke from another nap. She slept in fits and starts, grabbing short periods of sleep here and there, whenever her sheer exhaustion was just too much for her to bear anymore.

Sleeping was not something she wanted to do, not here. She didn't like the idea that she didn't know what was going on around her. She wanted to keep alert and awake.

But it was nearly impossible. He kept pumping her full of drugs, making her delirious, making her question what was real and what was a nightmare.

Whenever possible, she fought him, made it difficult for him, but he'd just hit her or threaten her with a knife. The one time she'd struggled while the needle was in, had led to a nasty wound in her arm. She'd not done that again.

She sat up to find the room in darkness, but something was different.

Something was wrong.

"Hello?"

She wasn't alone, she could feel it, someone's eyes, watching her.

Squinting, she peered into the shadows, hunting for signs that someone was there, only to have a figure step from the far wall, into the faint light coming from the single small window.

"I wonder if you're more trouble than you're worth," he said. "I might kill you tomorrow, put you out in the garden with the others and find someone new."

Without another word, the figure turned and walked out, leaving her with a gnawing terror deep inside as she contemplated what was to come.

28

Standing on the side of the street, Yana pulled her coat tighter to keep the cold out while she waited. It had been a long shot, calling them, but as it turned out, they seemed pleased to have heard from her, and quickly arranged a meeting.

She'd arrived early and kept checking the time on her phone until finally, the glossy black car pulled up, and the rear passenger door opened. Inside, a man looked up at her and then scooted over to the far side of the back seat.

"Get in," he said in a broad Russian accent.

Yana checked the street one last time. No one seemed to be taking much interest in them, but then the threat was most likely going to be inside the car, not out here on the street.

The dark interior of the vehicle loomed before her, and for a brief moment, she considered turning and walking away, but she quickly discounted that idea. She was well aware of who she was dealing with here, and the Russian Mafia did not take kindly to people wasting their time.

Steeling her nerves, she stepped into the car and sat down, closing the door behind her.

"So, Yana. It is a pleasure to finally meet you. Vassili has mentioned you before."

"Favourably, I hope?"

"I did not expect your phone call. I had thought that maybe you had been taken in along with Vassili."

"No. I wouldn't allow that to happen. Vassili thinks he is immune to the law, but I know better."

"I'm glad to hear it Yana, because Vassili has outlived his usefulness, and as of tomorrow, I will be cutting him loose. Jacob and the others too. We're cutting our losses."

"The police have witnesses."

"We know," the man replied. "The girls are of no consequence to us. We can find more girls."

"And me?" Yana asked, suddenly worried that this could be her end. She glanced to her left at the two silent figures in the front seats, before looking back at the man beside her. He smiled.

"You?" he said, regarding her with appraising eyes. "No, I have plans for you. I am impressed with your skills, Yana. Skills that will work well for us."

Yana breathed a sigh of relief. "What do you have in mind?"

29

"How did you sleep?" Kate asked.

"Alright, actually," Jon replied, thinking back to the night before and how he'd sent Sydney on her way. After that, he'd managed to get into bed and slip into a deep slumber that had actually resulted in a proper night's rest.

He felt grateful for these small mercies.

"Good, so you're rested and ready to get going then?"

Jon nodded as he sat at the table in the incident room, his team filing in for the morning briefing and update.

"What's this I hear about 'Finger-Girl?'" Rachel asked.

"Finger-Woman, and Gravy-Man," Kate replied, correcting her.

"You know that sounds all kinds of wrong, right?"

"It's so wrong, it's right," Jon said, nodding his head.

"No, just wrong. Very, very wrong."

"I don't want any part of your gravy… sir," Dion said.

"Or your finger," Rachel added, with a raised eyebrow at Kate.

Jon put on a deep, gravelly voice. "Gravy-Man considered the words of his trusty sidekicks but found them to be small-minded and petty. Gravy-Man was only concerned with ending crime on the streets of Surreyburg, and bringing justice to the people."

"I think he's finally lost it," Rachel said.

"It's sad to see," Dion added. "He'll be fondly remembered."

"I think fondly is a little strong. Maybe just remembered?"

"Occasionally thought about?" Dion suggested.

"Or referenced?"

"Oi, Dion, smart arse, tell me what you've got, or you'll feel the wrath of..." he put on the deep voice again, "...Gravy-Man."

"*That* is a scary thought," Dion replied, glancing at Rachel.

"Terrifying," she agreed. "I think you should do as the crazy man asks."

"Good idea. Right, well, I got the phone records of Russell, Blake, and most of his staff, and started going through them. I couldn't find Sydney's, though."

"That's okay," Jon replied, unconcerned about her for the moment. "What did you find?"

Dion sighed. "Nothing. Not a thing. No suspicious activity at all."

"And you're sure you had the right people?"

"They were the records for their contract phones, yes. Which obviously doesn't cover landlines or burner phones. So it's hardly comprehensive."

"No, not really. What about the CCTV from the Dance Fever Club?"

"I've only just got it, and I'm going through it now. Hopefully, I'll have something for you before too long."

"Good man. We'll make a sidekick out of you yet."

"Oh, I'm so happy," he replied, his voice flat and emotionless, giving Rachel side-eye.

She smirked.

"Anything to report, Rachel?"

"I'm afraid not," she answered. "Jacob is still missing, with no sign of him so far, and there's been no sightings of Olivia either."

"Kate?"

"Zack, Tyler, and Vassili were singularly unhelpful yesterday. We didn't really get anything out of them. The girl we picked up is still in a bad way in hospital, but we might get to talk to her today. She's under guard by uniformed police round the clock too."

"Nathan, tell me you have some better news."

He smiled. "Actually, I think I do."

"Oh?" Jon replied, perking up.

"Okay, so I kept on hunting, looking for that case I mentioned of the girl who went missing under similar circumstances to Olivia. I was sure I hadn't imagined it, and it turns out, I was right. This one was nearly a year ago. A girl called Maya Reid, who had no prior link to Russell at all. She was young, still in her teens, and was out clubbing with her friends when they started hanging out with Russell and his entourage one night. The evening went smoothly, and Maya went home, only for her to disappear a few days later. There were other leads in the case other than Russell, of course. In fact, Russell was a very minor one, and everyone who'd been out, including Russell, had an alibi for the time of her kidnapping. So that line of enquiry died a death right there."

"I'm guessing they never found her?"

"You guessed correctly. The case is still technically ongoing, but they don't have any leads."

"Right, I think there's something to this. Two missing persons were suspicious, although probably coincidental, but three? I don't know what's going on here, but something isn't right."

"I agree," Nathan replied. "Also, I'm willing to bet that if I kept digging, hunting through old files, I'd find more. In fact, I kind of want to."

"For now, go ahead. I see no reason not to keep looking. The more proof we have against him the better. Good work—"

"Actually," Nathan interrupted. "There was one other thing I think you should be aware of."

"There's more?"

"After Alan got locked up, I've had a friend in the prison keep an eye on his visitors. Over the last few years, he's let me know when anyone comes to see him. Turns out, he had another visitor last night."

"Another?" For a moment, Jon felt perplexed, and then a terrible thought occurred. Oh no.

"Yep," Nathan continued. "A woman paid him a visit claiming to be on his legal team. She needed urgent access and had ID on her. But my friend got suspicious and looked into it. He couldn't find anything obviously wrong, but things didn't add up. So he sent me a CCTV print out of her."

Nathan placed a sheet of paper on the table, and everyone stood to get a better look. Sure enough, Jon's suspicions were confirmed.

It was Sydney.

"How the hell?"

"My thoughts exactly," Nathan replied. "What on earth was she doing going to see Alan? I mean, I know she's with Russell, so maybe she has links to the group Russell belongs to? And if that's the case, then access to him isn't that unlikely. But still, why? And why her?"

Jon listened as he thought back to her visit the night before, and some of the things she said. So, that was the lead she mentioned? Why would she go to see Alan? How on earth could that help her?

As he started to think it through, his phone began to vibrate in his pocket. Plucking it out, it said it was a withheld number. He frowned.

"Are you going to answer that?" Kate asked.

"Um, yeah, hold on," he replied, and left the room, putting the phone to his ear as he walked to his office. "Hello?"

"Good morning, Jon," Sydney said on the other end of the line. "It's a bright and lovely day, is it not?"

"How on earth did you get in to see Alan?" he asked, stepping into his office and shutting the door behind him.

"You know, it's amazing what you can do with the right ID, contacts, and a bit of money."

"What the hell were you doing there? What are you playing at?"

"I told you I had a lead, Jon. I wasn't kidding."

"But Alan?"

"He was quite talkative, once I laid out my plan. He quite liked it, really, and then he was really very forthcoming, a joy to speak to, actually. He had what I needed, and now the deed is done."

"What are you talking about?"

"You'll find out soon enough. In the meantime, I suggest you get to Russell as soon as you can. I think you'll find him more than ready to talk," she replied, and then hung up.

Jon pulled the phone away from his ear and stared at it for several long moments before putting it back in his pocket. They needed to get to Russell, and luckily, with Nathan coming through with the second case, they had a really good reason to go there.

Was Russell the kidnapper? Would they find Olivia finally? Jon strode out of the office and made for the incident room. They needed to get going.

30

"What the hell do you think she was playing at, going to see Alan?" Kate asked. "Who is she? I didn't take her to be a lawyer."

"Neither did I," Jon replied as they drove through the Surrey landscape into Kingswood, towards Russell's estate. "I think that was just her cover. As for what she was doing there, I'm not sure. But I don't trust her."

"Damn right."

"At least Nathan had the foresight to keep tabs on him."

What had Alan given her, he wondered, and how might this affect their hunt for Olivia? Hopefully, it wouldn't affect the hunt at all, or maybe it would even help them.

"I think it's all linked to Russell, somehow," Kate said. "The other cases of missing girls, his girlfriend meeting with Alan, it's all very suspicious."

Jon nodded. He had to admit, it didn't look good for Russell, and as they turned into the driveway of Russell's house and saw the front gates smashed in, he realised just how right she might be.

Kate picked up the pool car's radio and pressed the button. "Look lively, guys. Looks like something's up."

"I see it," an officer in the patrol car behind replied. "What do you want to do?"

Jon considered his options as he slowed the car for a moment and glanced in the rearview mirror at the police car behind them. "We go in," he replied and gunned the engine. He had no idea what they were going to find. Someone like Russell probably had more than a few enemies, so they'd need to be careful.

Speeding up the long driveway, they soon reached the front of the house to find a beat-up looking car abandoned at the end of a series of skid marks on the tarmac.

Jon jumped out and grabbed his stab vest from the back. Kate did the same, and they threw them on as they formed up with the pair of uniformed officers and strode towards the entrance.

"I don't recognise the car," Kate said. "It's not a flashy one."

"No," Jon agreed, and stepped up to it and peered inside. The interior of the car was a mess, with used food cartons and rubbish everywhere. There was a blanket in the back too. Had the owner been sleeping in here?

"Look," Kate said, pointing through the window without touching it. "Someone's been doing research on Russell."

Following her gaze, Jon could make out printed-off maps of the local area with notes scribbled on them, several of which mentioned the name, Russell.

Someone had been very keen to find him, and it looked like they were inside. Was Sydney inside with him? Were they both in trouble? Ahead, the open front door loomed large.

Where was Blake, Russell's security guy? Surely he should be here?

With his stab vest in place, he grabbed his baton and extended it with a flick.

"Police," Jon shouted as he stepped cautiously through the doorway. "We're coming in."

Jon heard a scuffle, movement, and some grunts from a room to his right.

He inclined his head towards the door, and Kate nodded her understanding as they set off across the entrance hall. As they neared the door, the living room where they'd first interviewed Russell came into view. Towards the middle, Russell struggled against the grip of a man Jon had only seen in mug shots.

Jacob.

He had his arm around Russell's neck, and a gun jammed up against his temple.

Crap, why is it always guns? Jon thought.

"Don't come any closer," Jacob called out.

Replacing his baton, Jon raised his hands. "I only want to talk."

"No, get lost. *I* need to talk to Russell, *alone*."

"We can't do that," Jon replied. "We can't leave you with him."

"Let me go... Ow," Russell hissed as Jacob pressed the gun into his temple.

"Shut it, you."

"Why are you here, Jacob?" Jon asked, keen to distract him and keep him talking.

"Because of this little shit bag."

"Why? What's he done?"

"He's got Olivia, and he's going to tell me where I can find her."

"I don't."

"You do, stop lying."

"Jacob," Jon called out. "What makes you think he has her?"

"Because he was flirting with her at the club. I saw the photo Lily took. I know what he was doing."

"No, it's not me. I was ju—" Russell hissed.

"Shut it. Unless you're going to tell me where she is, be quiet."

Something clicked inside Jon's head in that instant, like a puzzle piece falling into place. Russell wasn't lying, he was sure of it. Russell didn't have Olivia, because Blake did.

He was suddenly sure of it.

He'd been the one to take Olivia's number, he was the one with two phones, and he also wasn't here to protect Russell. Did Sydney know this? Did Russell?

He thought back to the other cases, and he was willing to bet that Blake had been present at the cases of the two girls Nathan had uncovered too.

"Hey," Jon said. "What if he doesn't know? What if you're wrong." He needed to get Jacob to put the gun down and let Russell go."

"No, it's him. I know it."

"Why? How?"

"Why else would she leave me? For his money, that's why. That's why she left me."

Jon grimaced. That was an incredibly shallow view of Olivia.

"She's just like all the other girls, all they want is our money."

And just like that, he'd generalised it across the whole gender.

"But Jacob, you hit her, didn't you? You abused her and hurt her. Do you think maybe *that* might have something to do with it?"

"Shut up!"

"What if you're wrong, Jacob? What if she's not here? Are you going to shoot him for no reason? You know how that will end, right?"

"But, he did…"

"I didn't," Russell protested. "I promise you, I didn't."

"Jacob," Jon said. "We're looking for her, and you have my word we will not stop until we have her."

"But… I… I just want to find her. I miss her," he pleaded, his voice cracking.

Jon could see him starting to relax his grip. "That's it, just let him go. You need to leave this to us. We will find her, I promise."

"But, what if you don't?"

"We will."

"Shit…" Jacob pulled his arm away from around Russell's neck, and then pushed him. He fell forward to land on his front.

"Put the gun down," Jon called out.

Jacob sighed, nodded, and threw it onto a nearby sofa, much to Jon's relief.

The uniformed officers ran forward and grabbed him. Jacob didn't resist and allowed himself to be cuffed without a struggle as Russell got to his feet.

Kate rushed to Russell's side and helped him sit in a chair. Jon walked towards Jacob. "You did the right thing, but you're coming with us."

"I know. But, do I have your word you'll find Olivia?"

Jon found it odd that this abuser could care for the girl he was hurting in what sounded like an honest way. But then, maybe when your mind was so warped, this was how you expressed your love for someone. He wasn't sure he'd ever really understand it, and he kind of never wanted to, either. For right now, though, keeping Jacob calm was probably the right way to go. "Sure. We'll find her. Right now, it's my highest priority. I'm not looking to do anything else."

"Thank you," Jacob replied. He sounded genuine. Did the guy have actual feelings towards Olivia? If so, he had a damn funny way of showing them.

The two uniformed officers, who'd now bagged the gun, led Jacob out of the house leaving Jon and Kate with Russell who was sitting in one of his chairs looking strung out. He had his head back, and his eyes closed, apparently catching his breath. With that moment of excitement over, Jon turned his attention to finding Olivia. He needed to talk to Russell, and he needed the man to answer honestly.

"Are you okay, Mr Hodges?" Jon asked, taking the sympathetic route.

"I think so," he replied and looked up. "That was... intense."

"It certainly was," Jon said not wanting to sympathise with this man any more than he needed to. He was a prime suspect, but they needed him to talk, especially if his theory about Blake was true.

"They say your whole life flashes before your eyes in situations like that," Russell said.

"And did it?" Kate asked.

"I'm not sure it was my whole life, but it did make me think." Russell frowned, and then looked up at them. "Why are you here? I mean, you can't have known that this crazy man was coming here today, could you?"

"No. We didn't—"

"In fact," Russell cut in, "I'm glad you're here, I need to talk to you."

"And we need to talk to you, too," Jon replied, keen to run through the cases with him and see what he knew. "You say you had nothing to do with Olivia's disappearance, but—"

"Well—"

"Mr Hodges, with respect, let me finish, please."

Russell nodded and shut his mouth.

"As I was saying, you claim you had nothing to do with Olivia's disappearance, and I might even believe you," he felt Kate's eyes on him suddenly, "but we've found evidence that links you to two previous cases of missing women so far, and we think there might be more. Firstly, Iryna Polka, a Polish woman who worked for you, who went missing under mysterious circumstances. The second, Maya Reid, was a teenager, like Olivia, who went missing after a night out with you, and your... friends. Now, I don't know about you, but one instance could be a coincidence. Two? Well, that's suspicious, sure, but still within the realms of possibility. But three? Now things are starting to look bad, Mr Hodges. These direct links, two of which are almost identical, are downright suspicious. Wouldn't you agree?"

"I know how it looks. I do. But I'm a wealthy socialite, someone with money and power, so I tend to attract attention."

"That's fair enough, but my point still stands. It's suspicious."

"Things will go much easier for you if you'd just be honest with us," Kate added.

"That's the thing," he answered, with a slightly amused smile. "I am being honest. I can show you where I was those days in my diary and provide you with witnesses. I can

231

promise you that I was not involved in those girls going missing, but I think I know who was."

"You know?" So he did know, interesting.

"I do. I think I do, anyway. I've come to suspect it more recently, and I'm happy to tell you."

"I'm sure any judge would look favourably upon you if you were to lead us to the right person."

"I'm going to be charged, am I?"

"That depends on whether it's determined you knew for a while, and were protecting him. But that's not for me to decide."

"Well, shit. This day just gets better and better."

"Are you going to tell us?" Kate asked.

"Yes, yes," he said with a sigh.

"No need, I think I know who it is. It's Blake, isn't it?

"Your security guy?" Kate asked

"Err, yeah, how did you know?" Russell asked, perplexed.

"We have CCTV footage of him taking Olivia's number, he's not here today to protect you, and I'm willing to bet he was with you when you met Maya too, right?"

"That's right. He was interested in Iryna too. I remember him fixating on her, almost to the point of obsession. I didn't think much of it back then but... He's been distant these last few days. He's not been around half the time and got offended when I quizzed him about it. That, and the fact that you came to me about Olivia, another girl going missing while he was in my employ. Like you say, three times is just a little too suspicious."

"Do you know where he has her?"

"Maybe. I think I have an idea. He bought a house that he thinks I don't know about. But I make a point of knowing as much as I can about the people who work closely with me, and I know about the house he owns in the countryside. It would make the perfect place to hide someone. They could scream all they liked, and no one would know."

"And where is this house?"

"I don't know the address by heart, but I can find it on a map. I know where it is."

"Here, show me on my phone," Kate said, opening Google Maps and handing it to him to navigate to the right place. He checked it on Satellite View, and then on Street View, before handing it back.

"That's it," he said.

"Are you sure?" Jon asked, looking at the view of the property from the road, displayed on the screen.

"Positive."

"And he's there now, with Olivia?"

"If it's him, and I'm positive it is, that's where they'll both be."

"Why didn't you come to us sooner?" Jon asked.

"I… I wasn't sure, and… I've just had a bit of a wake-up call."

"Well, I hope it hasn't come too late. Stand up please."

"Wait, why?" Russell asked.

"We're taking you in, Mr Hodges. We have way more questions to ask you, and we'll be doing it at the station."

"Oh, well, I guess that's okay."

"It had better be," Jon replied and took Russell by the arm to lead him out of the building. Another police car had already appeared, and they were able to hand Russell over to them right away.

Jon made to head back to his car, and then stopped, and looked back at Russell.

"One other thing," he asked. "Where's Sydney?"

Russell's eyes turned cold at the sound of her name. "She left, yesterday. I have no idea where that bitch is."

"That's a little harsh…"

"You would be too if you were in my position," he replied, and turned away, apparently done with the conversation. Nearby, Kate had already started the car up. Hopefully, it was time to end this, he thought, as he jumped into the passenger seat.

31

"Do you know where you're going?" Jon asked as Kate raced along the country roads, leaving the suburban area of Kingswood behind.

"Yeah," Kate replied. "It's in Headley, on one of the roads going through there. There's a bunch of random, isolated houses that way."

"Where no one would hear her if she made a fuss."

"Yep," Kate replied. "If he's telling the truth."

"You think he isn't?"

"Do you trust him?"

"Well, no, of course not, in general. But on this. I don't know. I think there's something to it. I mean, we have him, right? It's not as if we've let him go, is it? So, why lie? Why throw your trusted security guy under the bus, if he's innocent?"

"Okay, fair point. It's going to be all over the news tomorrow that he's been arrested. His reputation is crumbling around him, so I guess he doesn't have much to lose by telling us the truth as he sees it. In fact, if he's right, this might actually save him some face. He could turn this into a positive."

"Yeah," Jon remarked, finding the idea to be a troubling one. "I'm not sure I like that idea. He could use this to whitewash himself."

"But, if he's right, then he's helped us solve the case."

"As much as it annoys me to admit it, yeah, he has. And yet, why do I feel like we've been out-manoeuvred all of a sudden?"

"Probably because we have. I don't trust Russell at all. He's a slimeball, but a cunning one."

"Aye up, hold on," Jon remarked as he pulled his vibrating phone from his pocket. It was the station. "Yup?"

"Guv, I thought you'd want to know," Dion replied. "I've been going through the CCTV from the club, and there's footage on there showing Russell's security guy, Blake, taking Olivia's number."

"You're sure?"

"One hundred percent."

"Right, good work."

"That's not all."

"Of course it isn't, why would it be?"

"Um, something the matter, sir?" Dion asked.

"No, nothing, Dion. It's just this case, it's doing my head in. Go on, what have you got?"

"In the footage, Blake is clearly seen handling two phones."

"Which is why you didn't find anything on the records you pulled," Jon replied, expanding on the revelation.

"Right."

"OK, cool. We're on our way to find Blake now, so hopefully, we'll have some good news for you shortly."

"Do you want backup?"

"We've called some in already," Jon replied. "Thanks."

"No worries," Dion replied. "Go get him."

Jon hung up and explained what Dion had found.

"I think that just about confirms it, then," Kate remarked. "Blake's our man."

"I hope so, I really do. And I hope she's still alive."

Kate nodded and accelerated. Jon hung on. They needed to get there as soon as possible.

Ten minutes later, they approached the building. It was an older house, off to their right, surrounded by fields without any other homes around.

"Russell wasn't kidding about how isolated it is," Jon said.

"I'm going to block the driveway," Kate replied.

"Go for it."

As they got closer, Kate slowed. She veered right pulling off the road into the driveway entrance at an angle, blocking it off completely. Anyone trying to run would need to do some serious damage to both cars to get out.

Jon jumped out and realised he'd need to get over the bonnet to walk up the driveway.

"Wait, wait. I've always wanted to do this," he said and took a running jump at the car as he attempted to slide over the bonnet like Starsky or Hutch.

The slide went surprisingly well, but the landing, not so much. Stumbling, he went arse-over-tit and landed awkwardly.

"Aww, I think I landed on my keys."

"Twat," Kate muttered.

"Don't just stand there, help me up."

She rolled her eyes and offered her hand. "Deary me, Gravy-Boy."

"Yeah, alright. Shut it," he replied and rubbed his hip. "That's gonna leave a mark."

"Come on," Kate urged. Jon got moving, figuring the best thing was to work it off as he ran. They jogged up the driveway, noting the large 4x4 as they approached the house.

"What's the plan?" Kate asked. "There's bound to be a rear door."

"Almost certainly."

"Want to wait for backup?"

"Hell no. I want Olivia out of there as quickly as possible. How about I take the back door, and you the front?"

Kate nodded. "Sounds like a plan."

Jon reached into his pocket for his device. "Grab your phone, put it on silent." She did as he asked, then he called her, and she picked up. "Keep in touch."

She moved off, and Jon went looking for a way around the back. Keeping low, he ducked under windows, peeking inside a few of them. Halfway round, through a side window, he saw a shadowy figure move out of one of the rooms and disappear from sight.

Blake was in the building. Or, someone was, he couldn't be sure without a better look.

"I just saw movement in the house," Jon said over the open line.

"Copy that."

He hoped Russell hadn't just sent them to a random house, and they weren't about to scare the pants off some poor unsuspecting guy.

Pressing on, Jon made his way around the building, ducking past more windows, and in one case, a set of patio doors at the back that led to an outside seating area. Just past that, he found the real back entrance.

"I'm at the door. I'm going to try it."

"Careful."

"Have you tried the front door?"

"Yeah, it's locked."

"Shit. Okay, wait a moment," he replied and reached out. Quietly turning the handle, the door suddenly swung loosely on its hinges. "Mine's open."

"Lucky you."

"I'm moving inside, I want to catch him off guard."

"I'll come around to you."

"No, wait there in case he runs. I'll come to you."

"Please be careful, Jon," she replied, a clear note of concern in her voice.

"I will." He pushed the door open. Slipping inside, he found himself in a utility room, with discarded shoes and coats beside a washer and dryer.

Moving up, Jon crept to an open door that led to the kitchen. Inching forward with his baton in one hand and phone in the other, he peered into the room.

Empty.

Breathing a sigh of relief, he stepped into the room, placing each foot down as quietly as he could. So far, the going was clear. A door at the far side of the room led deeper into the house. He couldn't see much from his current position and took a few more steps.

His heart worked overtime, beating like a drum against his ribs as adrenaline surged through his system. Part of him wanted to turn and run out right that second and wait for backup, but he couldn't. Something about the feel of the place made him stay. He felt sure Olivia was here somewhere. Probably upstairs in a bedroom, or the attic. Maybe in the basement.

Approaching the door, he leant forward, looking into a hallway with doors on either side, and another at the end. He took another step, only for a shadowy figure to step out from a side room and cross the hall.

Jon ducked back on reflex and heard his foot scuff the floor.

Shit, he cursed in his mind, hoping the man hadn't heard him. He tensed. He couldn't see up the hall from where he was, so held his baton ready in case the man appeared.

Nothing.

Focusing on his breathing, Jon calmed himself down and edged forward once more. The hallway was clear and the house was silent once more.

Was that him? Was that Blake? He couldn't be sure. It was a man, he felt confident about that, and he looked about the right size. But he'd ducked back so quickly he'd not really managed to get a good look at him.

Damn, he needed to know for sure, and he needed Kate in here.

Jon took another calming breath and set off up the hallway, looking for anything like a set of keys, just in case he needed to unlock the door, but he couldn't see anything.

Partway up, Jon reached the door on the left and looked inside. The room was deserted, but he recognised it as the place he'd first seen the shadow. He could see the window he'd looked in through too, and realised how clearly you could see outside.

Had the man seen him?

A fresh wave of worry and fear blew through him as he wondered how on earth he'd managed to put himself in this situation. He shook his head and pressed on, passing a set of stairs leading up, and another door on his right. The man had gone that way, but there was no sign of him now.

Jon bit on the inside of his cheek in consternation, but continued up the hallway. Beyond it, an entrance hall opened up as Jon inched through the door. Ahead, he saw a couple of steps leading up to the main front door, complete with a deadbolt.

With a final glance back, Jon reached out, gripped the knob and twisted. But the door held fast.

"Crap," he hissed and flicked the bolt open with his thumb against the catch.

Footsteps sounded behind him, approaching fast. Jon ducked. Something solid hit his back. "Aaagh."

"Jon?" Kate called out.

Turning, he saw Blake lunge at him again. He swung a wooden bat. Jon raised his arm, and Blake caught his shoulder. It was a bloody cricket bat.

Crying out, Jon launched himself at the man, his arm burning with pain. "Kate, get in here," he shouted.

"I'm coming."

Going for the bat, Jon grabbed it and tried to yank it from him. He forced Blake back, who then tripped, and Jon fell on top. Behind him, there was a bang on the door as Kate kicked it. And then again.

With a tug, he tried to pull the bat from Blake's grasp, but he held fast.

Kate kicked the door again.

"Blake, stop this," Jon called out.

"No. I'm gonna cave your head in, pig." He jerked the bat. The grip caught Jon the face, and he saw stars. The loss in concentration cost him as he let go of the bat. Blake pushed up, and Jon fell back. "And then, I'm gonna do that partner of yours."

Bang, on the door again.

"Sounds like she's desperate to see me," Blake taunted.

Cursing, Jon knew he'd left himself open. Blake lashed out with a right hook and caught his cheek.

"Aaagh," Jon yelped as pain bloomed up the left side of his face. On his knees, he shuffled back. Blake swung the bat low and buried it in his sternum.

His wind left him entirely as he fought to catch his breath. Blake moved around him as Jon leant forward, putting his hand on the floor, as he tried to suck in some air with ragged gasps.

The door shook, bending on his hinges as Kate kicked again.

Finally, Jon sucked in a long wheezing breath. Then, with a move he didn't follow, Blake suddenly had the bat up under Jon's neck. Standing behind him, he pulled, and Jon felt his airway close.

He couldn't breathe.

Frantically, he grabbed the bat, clawing at it with his fingers as he fought for some air, any air.

Blake pulled on the bat, jamming it up under his jaw.

Oxygen, he needed oxygen. Desperately trying to pull the bat away, adrenaline forced him to fight for his life. He couldn't go out like this.

But there wasn't any air. He might as well have been at the bottom of the ocean because there was nothing. The muscles in his chest spasmed as he felt his vision start to tunnel, and the fight faded from him.

Darkness closed in, and he felt like he could hear someone calling to him, calling his name in the endless darkness.

Was it Charlotte? Would he see her again?

That wouldn't be so bad...

Light blazed before him, blinding him, and a shadow moved. All he could hear was his blood pumping in his ears, making the world around him seem muffled by comparison. Something jerked. It sounded like he was underwater.

Suddenly he fell. Life-giving air rushed into his lungs as he took several laboured breaths.

"Jon?"

Who was that? Charlotte? Kate? His vision swam. Blinking, he cleared the tears from his eyes and saw Kate leaning over him. He was alive, and Blake wasn't trying to kill them.

Relief flooded through him.

"Jon?"

"It's Gravy-Man to you," he said between coughs.

"Oh, do piss off," she groaned and pulled him up.

Sitting upright, he looked over to see Blake on the floor, moaning, his head several teeth lighter than it had been, and blood leaking from his mouth.

"Wow..." Jon muttered as Kate moved over to the supine man. She turned him over, then proceeded to cuff him and read him a police caution, arresting him for suspected kidnapping. "You did that?"

With Blake secure, she smiled back at him. "I was the star batter in my rounders team at school. Comes in handy from time to time."

"No shit."

Jon heard sirens outside, as he noted the bloody baton on the floor and the kicked-in door. She must have come charging through and swung at him as if she was going for a home run. He wished he'd seen that, he was willing to bet it looked magnificent.

Moments later, Jon was getting to his feet, and two uniformed officers came running into the house.

"Deal with him, please," Kate said, and looked over at Jon, holding a small key in her hand. "Look what I found in Blake's back pocket."

"Looks like a handcuff key," Jon muttered, still not feeling quite with it.

"Let's go find Olivia, shall we?"

"Oh, yeah," Jon replied, suddenly desperate to find her.

He nodded, feeling like he was getting some of his strength back, and followed Kate. They checked the last of the rooms downstairs, but found little of interest, and headed upstairs. All the rooms upstairs were empty too, but eventually, they found a second staircase leading up to a converted attic room. The door at the top was locked, and the key she'd recovered from Blake was too small to fit.

"Screw this," Kate muttered and kicked it.

The old wooden door shook, then buckled on the second kick as wood splintered.

"I'm getting the hang of this," she said as she delivered her third kick, and the door flew open to reveal a squalid room beyond, and a terrified Olivia on a single dirty bed. It was the only piece of furniture apart from a bucket on the floor.

Jon watched as Kate ran over and used the key to free Olivia's cuffed wrists, and then pull her in for a hug. With his neck, shoulder, and ribs still aching, Jon sank to the floor and rested his head against the door frame, thankful it was over.

"It's okay. You're safe now," Kate reassured Olivia, who hugged her tight and started to cry.

Despite the pain, Jon felt a keen sense of relief that they'd found Olivia. She was hurting and would live with this for the rest of her life, but she was alive, and that was everything.

32

Leaning back in the soft seat, Jon winced as his ribs touched the cushion. The pain was greatly reduced, but still there.

The restaurant buzzed around him as people talked and laughed, enjoying their meals and having a good time. Rachel had done well, the Ivy was a lovely restaurant. The prices were a little eye-watering, but the food was to die for.

He'd happily eat here for the rest of his life if he could afford it.

Kate had just nipped to the bathroom, leaving Jon alone for a moment. As he waited, he pulled out his phone and checked the news reports. Scrolling down, he suddenly spotted one of interest and opened it up. It was a typically salacious report, talking about Russell Hodges, who was, it said, apparently arrested today in connection to the recent case of the missing girl.

The story went on to detail how it turned out that one of Mr Hodges' staff, a security guard, had been arrested for her kidnapping and assault. According to their sources, Russell himself noted his employee's strange behaviour and reported him.

Russell was being hailed as some kind of hero for this, but there was some bad news too. The report went on to detail how Russell had suddenly lost millions on an unspecified bad business deal earlier in the day, causing shares in RH Enterprises to plummet, only for them to recover somewhat following the news of him helping the police.

The report went on to say how this particular news organisation hoped the local philanthropist would bounce back soon.

But Jon was more interested in the bad business deal. Reading between the lines, he felt sure that there was a lot more to it than was being reported, and in fact, was not a bad business deal at all.

No, he thought, this sounded like Sydney. She'd somehow swindled millions from Russell, blackmailed him, and then left him in the lurch. With a slow shake of his head, he turned off the screen on his phone as he spotted Kate threading her way through the tables, back to him. She looked like another woman entirely in a green dress with her hair down.

"You alright?" she asked, retaking her seat.

"Yeah. I was just looking at a news report. It made out that it was Russell that did all the work in hunting Blake down."

"Of course they did," Kate remarked and shrugged. "They're just building a narrative that suits them. Maybe he's an investor of theirs."

Jon nodded. "Yeah, maybe..."

"Thank you for bringing me here. I've always wanted to try it out."

"You've heard good things?"

"Yeah!"

"Then I'm pleased to be able to indulge you."

"Thank you."

"You know, after the Alan thing, and you said you wanted to slow down, I thought you didn't want to... I thought you regretted having spent that night with me."

She smiled. "No. I don't regret it. But I just wasn't myself that week, what with the court case and everything. You know?"

"I understand."

"I think I just needed some... affection, maybe?"

"I'm just pleased you didn't write me off."

"No. But, I want to take it slow. I barely know you, Jon. But, this is nice."

He nodded, feeling a small spark of hope deep inside start to glow a little brighter.

"Don't be sad," she said.

"I'm not. Quite the opposite. I'm pleased."

"Good. We closed a case today, we got our man. You should be happy."

"I am. I mean, as happy as I can be, given he nearly killed me."

"I'm surprised nothing was broken," Kate said. "He really did a number on you. We didn't have to do this tonight you know. I could have waited."

"No, I wanted to. Besides, it's just sitting and talking. How hard can that be?"

"Well, as long as you're sure."

"So, did I miss anything while I was at the hospital?" he asked. He'd been there a while as they checked him out and made sure nothing was seriously wrong. While he was there, the chief had called and told him to go back to the hotel and rest for the remainder of the day. He hadn't felt like arguing, but after a few hours, he'd been restless and called Kate to make sure the date was still going ahead.

He was keen to see her and find out how the rest of the day had gone.

"You didn't miss much, no. Olivia's parents came by the station and took her home. I think she was actually pleased to go back with them in the end. From what she told us, she's been through a complete nightmare. We've referred her for some professional help, and I hope she takes it. I think she'll need it. Some of the things she was telling me were just horrific."

"Poor kid," Jon replied, feeling sorry for her. "I wish we could have found her sooner."

"I know. Me too. But it wouldn't have made much difference to her mental state. She'd been suffering through months of abuse, way before Blake ever got his hands on her."

"Some people just seem to go from one problem to the next in life."

Kate nodded. "Blake was just the icing on the cake. From what Olivia said, we think he would have killed her eventually. We've had a team going over the grounds of his house, and we've already found what we think are human remains."

"He abuses them, kills them, and buries them?"

"Basically."

"What an upstanding member of society."

"Tell me about it. He's not really talking much, and he's denying everything, but the evidence is already overwhelming. I can't see him wiggling out of this one."

"Not as long as Olivia gives evidence, no."

"Yeah. I think she will, but I guess you never really know."

"So, where did he kidnap her from?"

"A car park in Epsom. Olivia thought she'd been talking to Russell, when in fact it had been Blake the whole time. He'd directed her to a spot that wasn't covered by CCTV, snuck up and attacked her."

"Attacked her? But she knew who he was, surely she'd have gone willingly?"

"What can I say, sicko's gonna sicko, Jon. Maybe he got a thrill out of it? Wouldn't be the first time."

"Yeah, I guess. What about Jacob, Vassili, and the others?"

"They've been charged, so they'll have their time in court."

"So how did Jacob find Russell?"

"He did his research," Kate replied. "Trawled through the net looking for anything that could help him find the man. He said he narrowed it down to Kingswood easily enough from interviews, and then with photos and Google Maps and such, he got a fairly good idea of where he was, and so parked outside to confirm it. Then he just barged in."

"Was he the one who assaulted Geoff Cook?"

"He admitted to that too, yeah. They've all suddenly become much more talkative actually."

"Oh, why?" Jon asked, curious.

"I think Vassili lost his support from his Russian friends. The Mob lawyer stopped coming, and they had to use duty solicitors. Everything changed then."

"Bad day for them. And Russell?

"Russell's been released, we didn't really have much on him, and we've had pressure come down from the ACC to release him. He was not happy about Russell being accused."

"Why am I not surprised? Shit, that's messed up." He thought back to the discussion he'd had with Nathan in the records room, about Russell's name not being on the system. Maybe he was onto something there.

"That's not all, he's apparently appointed a new detective superintendent."

"I've got a new boss?"

She smiled. "I've not met them yet, but if they're loyal to Ward, I think we both know what kind of person we'll be dealing with."

"Yep, wonderful. Just what I wanted to hear. I suppose it'll be someone else we can all complain about though. So there's that."

"Every cloud," she replied and took a sip of her wine. Jon joined her, enjoying its fruity taste.

"So, here's a question I've been wondering about," Kate said. "Why do you think Russell suddenly handed Blake over? Do you really think it was for the optics?"

"I think it was Sydney," Jon replied, leaning forward on the table.

"Sydney?"

"Yeah, I didn't find a moment to talk to you before, but she paid me a visit last night. She just turned up at the hotel."

"What?"

"I know! I couldn't quite believe it. Anyway, she hinted that she was about to become a very rich woman. She also said she might be able to help with the case, but that she just had a lead to follow up first."

Kate looked away and frowned, before looking back a second later. "The prison visit. That was her lead."

Jon nodded. "I think Alan saw a way to get back at Russell and really screw him over. He clearly told Sydney something, something she could use to blackmail Russell and get her payday. And not only that, I think she suspected Blake, but knew that Russell knew, and told him to tell us."

"Wow," Kate replied. "I'm not sure I know what to think of her. I mean, it's great that she helped us, but I'm not sure I agree with her methods."

"Like you said, she's trouble. And just to add more weight to our theory, I just saw a news report saying that Russell lost millions in a bad business deal..."

"It was Sydney, wasn't it?"

"That would be my guess, yes."

"Holy crap."

"She's really got some balls," Jon agreed.

"Ovaries, Jon. She'd got some ovaries. Balls are fragile things, and she's clearly not that."

"No. No, she's not."

"So, why did she come to see you at the hotel? I mean, why tell you beforehand?"

"What can I say? It must be my magnetic personality." Jon shrugged and put some swagger into his voice. "Once you get a taste of this, nothing else is good enough."

"Oh, get over yourself, Gravy-Boy," Kate replied. "That's one hell of a story, though. So, she was out to swindle Russell all this time."

"Aye, and you know how she cornered me in that basement corridor at the station?" Jon asked.

"Yeah?"

"Well, I'd been talking to Nathan in the records room about his trip to see Alan, and how he thought Alan knew something about Russell, but wouldn't tell him. I think Sydney overheard that, realised that Alan could give her the leverage she needed, and went to see him."

"Oh, and he trusted her more than Nathan and told her what she needed to know..." Kate replied, tailing off.

"...In order to screw Russell over for getting him sent to prison," Jon added. "Because Sydney could do what we couldn't."

"Clever. Russell loses millions to her, and Alan gets one over on a rival." Kate frowned. "So, do you think she knew about Jacob going to attack Russell?"

"I don't think so," Jon replied, weighing the options in his head. "I think that was a coincidence."

A quizzical look passed over her face. "So, only one question remains."

"And what's that?"

"What did Russell do that was so bad, he paid millions to keep Sydney quiet?"

Jon sighed. "I don't know."

33

Jon lay on his bed in the hotel room, holding his phone above him, scrolling through his notifications. He looked over the email from the estate agent and smiled. His offer had been accepted on the house.

Finally, I'll have a home, he thought, as the phone suddenly vibrated in his hand.

He dropped it in surprise and it landed on his face with a *thunk*.

"Aaah, shit. Stupid bloody phone." Removing the device from his face, he saw a number he didn't recognise and was about to decline the call, but then reconsidered.

He answered.

"Hello?"

"Good evening, Jon," Sydney said.

"You again..."

"Naturally," she replied whimsically. "It's always lovely to hear your voice. I've taken quite the shine to you, you know."

"I'm so lucky," Jon replied sarcastically, a shiver running up his spine. A thought occurred to him. "I have a question."

"Ask away, handsome."

Jon's eye twitched. "When we arrived at Russell's house, he was being attacked by the missing girl's boyfriend. Did you know he was going to do that?"

She snorted. "Ha! No. I didn't. Fascinating. Deserved though, I think."

"I'm not sure I agree with you, Sydney."

"I think you should."

"Is Sydney even your real name?"

He could hear the smile in her voice as she replied. "You really are a true detective, aren't you, Pilgrim?"

"Well, is it?"

"No, it's not."

"Are you going to tell me your real name?"

"No, not yet. You'll have to earn that privilege, Jon. I'm not one to give away information for free. I think you should know that about me by now."

"Oh, I'm well aware. So why call?"

"I just wanted to offer my thanks. Russell turned out to be very profitable for me, in part because of you. So, thank you."

"I'm not sure I really want those thanks, so instead, maybe you can tell me what Russell did? Why'd he happily hand over millions to you?"

"Aaah, no. That one stays with me, I'm afraid. Sorry," she replied, apparently enjoying this verbal sparring match from the tone of her voice.

"I had to ask."

"Of course you did. I would expect nothing less from a consummate professional like yourself. Anyway, I've said what I wanted to. So, bye, Jon. I think I'll be seeing you soon enough." She hung up.

"Ugh, I hope not," Jon muttered and stared at his phone. On a whim, he then saved the contact, typing in *Evil Bitch*, as the name.

With a sigh, he let the phone fall to the bed as he stared up at the ceiling. As he considered her words, he spotted a spider in the corner of the room, busily wrapping a fly up in its web.

Why did he get the feeling that he was the fly, and Sydney was the spider?

THE END

Book 3
Silence of the Dead
On Amazon, here:
www.amazon.co.uk/dp/B08WPCWH56

Author Note

Thank you for reading book two of the Pilgrim Crime Thriller series, I really appreciate you taking the time to read my crazy stories.

Coming up with book two after finishing book one is never easy. I need to follow on from the previous book, continue the story, live up to what happened in the first, and also dive deeper into the characters. I hope I've managed to do that and deliver an engaging story.

Something that I'm keen to show is Jon's journey, and the differences he experiences as a northerner living down south, and I'll likely drip-feed these things in as the series progresses. But it is fun to write, especially as it's something I have personally experienced.

One of the big things in this book is the introduction of Sydney as an ongoing side character. I really enjoyed writing the scenes between her and Jon, and I really want to have her pop up from time to time in future books. She's fun to write.

As I write this, I've not yet come up with a plan for book three, but I'm sure by the time you're reading these words, there will be a third book ready for pre-order.

If you enjoyed this book, one thing that really helps is a review. It doesn't need to be anything more than just a quick sentence about how much you enjoyed it, but these small things help in a huge way.

Thanks again for reading A Tangled Web.

Kindest Regards,
A L Fraine.

www.alfraineauthor.co.uk

Printed in Great Britain
by Amazon